THE LEGENDS OF A STARTUP GUY

PRACHI GARG

Srishti
PUBLISHERS & DISTRIBUTORS

SHRISHTI PUBLISHERS & DISTRIBUTORS
Registered Office: N-16, C.R. Park
New Delhi – 110 019
Corporate Office: 212A, Peacock Lane
Shahpur Jat, New Delhi – 110 049
editorial@Shrishtipublishers.com

First published by
Shrishti Publishers & Distributors in 2019

Printed at Repro Knowledgecast Limited, Thane

Prachi Garg is an author, motivational speaker, and an entrepreneur. She is a founder of ghoomophiro.com, an enterprise that pioneers in women solo travel. She has been featured as top 10 Indian women, who made big online. She has authored the bestselling book Superwomen, that talks about the journeys of women entrepreneurs. The book has been constantly topping the non-fiction charts at various bookstores. Her book SuperCouples is about couple-preneurs and their journey of balancing the relationship and work. SuperSiblings is the third book in this series and captures the essence of siblings and a startup together. She has given several entrepreneurial talks in many educational institutions, including the IITs and IIMs.

Apart from being an MBA graduate from Great Lakes Institute of Management, Chennai, she is a distinguished alumna from Miranda House too.

The Legends of a Startup Guy is her attempt to foray into the world of fiction.

: /authorprachigarg   : @prachimadri

: @prachi1905

Happy Reading!!

loads of wishes

Prachi Garg

By the same author

Superwomen is an interesting journey of how twenty women entrepreneurs played all their roles to perfection, aligning their families with their ambitions, showing the world their true mettle.

SuperCouples brings out lovely stories of enterprising couples who break stereotypes and cover a varied range of services: ecommerce, innovative gifts, eco-friendly products, health care solutions, event management, digital solutions and many others.

Varying from tech start-ups to trendy fashion wear, from utility applications to artsy expressions, *SuperSiblings* encapsulates the journeys of twenty siblings supported each other to start-up their dream ventures.

*Dedicated to
my father Brejesh Garg,
and mother Neeru Garg.*

Acknowledgements

This book has been possible due to the enormous love and support that people have given to me. It was their constant support that kept me going and ensured that I should be able to deliver it on time. I would like to thank everyone for making the journey smooth for me.

Family members play a great role to make such accomplishments possible. In my case as well, this holds true. Each one of them has been instrumental and has been there when required.

Mr. Arup Bose from Shrishti Publishers for his faith in my concept and agreeing to publish the same.

Stuti, my editor, who undertook the tedious task of going through my manuscript, editing it and coming out with exciting ideas.

All my friends who provided me with constant moral support to make this happen.

All the readers of *Superwomen, SuperCouples* and *Supersiblings,* whose love inspired me to pen down *The Legends of a Startup Guy.*

Introduction

*T*his is not a story about a hero who rose from the shackles of a tough world. Neither is it a narrative about someone who grew up against challenges of financial crisis and built an empire of his own. This is a tale of someone who was born with a silver spoon, and yet, decided to write his own destiny, on his own terms and to bring meaning to his existence out of the shadows of his lineage.

Ganesha – an infant who was jovial, intelligent and the youngest in the family. A foodie by heart and lazy by nature, he always looked for ways to make life easier and more convenient. His elder sibling, Skanda, was an absolute favourite in the family and had been working as one of the top strategic technology builders of the world. Despite having everything, from financial strength, quality education to environment, Ganesha had to battle through immense identity crisis under the shadow of his very accomplished brother and parents.

A boy known best as social and always willing to find solutions in crisis, even as a kid, Ganesha was known for his management skills in case of dire emergency. No matter how gigantic the challenge was, the helpful soul always had a solution. "We never got to know if Ganesha was going through any trouble. He was simply so busy making sure that everything and everybody around him continued with life smoothly, that we would often wonder what was going on inside that mind of his to give him such infinite patience," Ganesha's mother, Parvati, speaks dotingly, claiming that her son clearly does not take after his father who is well-known for his temper. It was often said of the even-headed youngster that he would be the first one to come to anyone's aid when they were looking for help! It is with this rare amiability that Ganesha generously made friends and shared his privileges with those who asked, thus making himself extremely popular amidst his peer group. But what set him apart from his peer was his superhuman sincerity and humility with which he carried out his actions to the last stretch. "He really means everything he says, you know, if his mom would tell him to guard the door, he would guard it, no matter what! I have seldom seen young boys with that kind of commitment and strength to stand up for what they feel," his father Shiva declares. His unique attitude, out of the box responses for even the simplest questions and his little world of imagination where he spent most of his time with his pet rat Jumbo, were all traits that amused people tremendously. In all, the entire community would have thought that Ganesha, the boy born with a silver spoon, lives an enviable life of luxury and has nothing to be unstable about his platter of comfort.

However, to see into the mind of that young boy and to find out the reality of what went on in that maze would have blown off the entire mountain village where he lived. Under layers of perfection, benevolence and jovial extravaganza was a young boy battling to be found for who he really was.

1

The Making of an Entrepreneur

*T*his started way before I started sharing my story with people, or before I even had a story to talk about. To most, I was known as the boy with all the luxuries. Nothing could possibly be wrong with my life with an influential father, a caring mother and an accomplished brother. I was given the best of education, food, clothes and everything else I wanted in life. However, under these materialistic layers of satiation were my own clouds of apprehensions, doubts and insecurities that I never got to share with anyone. While I was surrounded by happiness externally, in my internal space, I was lonely and desperate. Under the warm and yet overbearing shadows of my parents, I was never expected to excel in anything. Nobody asked about my report cards, no stories of excellence were brought to me to compare. In fact, what really pinched my ego the most was that nobody even recognized my aspirations or the need to have them and never asked me what I wanted to be. It was almost like being good was the only quality I possessed. That was all I needed to continue doing and my folks would take care of the rest of the world for me. Eventually, though, I broke the silence. I wanted to be more than that. For the first time, I found my own thoughts reeking of incredulous determination and strength, reflecting on the amount of desperation I had felt in the years of my youth to break out of the cocoon.

The beginning of the metamorphosis, both external and internal, began when I was still a teenager. I watched my elder brother Skanda leave home to become a professional engineer in one of the most reputed organizations of the country. The amount of praise he received, the number of 'well-wishers' who came to meet before he left and all this, contrasted to how inconspicuous I was made to feel in the shadows of this accomplishment was something that flicked a switch in me. That night, I remember, I did not sleep. With Jumbo fiddling around his play box, I watched the little rodent scurry from one part of his play room to another. And all this while, in my head, I replayed every word said to my brother, the beaming smile on my parents' face and the weight of invisibility I felt under all that ignorance.

"I am not being jealous," I spoke to Jumbo, like I always did while floating in my own world. "But I don't think I will ever get to experience that elation or watch mom and dad be so proud of me. Nobody expects to me do anything."

I remember distinctly how Jumbo had paused for a minute to watch me, his dear friend as though he totally understood everything I was telling him, and then went about making his way through the large array of objects scattered around him. It was then that I started noticing what he really was doing. Jumbo did not seem to be bothered by the size of obstacles in front of him; his heart was set on my plate of snacks lying at the top of the table. Although the little one knew very well that I would eventually share the treat with him anyway, he was determined to get there on his own, and he did! I watched all this with great interest. I had not expected a rat to be so sentimental about his aspirations or ever thought he would be willing to set out on a journey; so difficult to achieve even for the smallest of treasures that were so accessible for him anyway. I think it was in that moment that something moved inside me. Maybe this entire time, it wasn't the world that had taken me for granted, but really it was I who was taking this beautiful and abundant world for granted. It was then that I knew that it was time to change. With that fired up determination, I began to burn the midnight oil and picked up my computer syllabus for the submissions I had due in the coming week. Ordinarily, I would have simply come up with one of my last minute creative ideas and produce a short cut document, just enough to seek myself a respectable source. But that trend had been broken. Like my rat, I was certain that from now on, I would battle for the highest point that was possible to achieve and prove my worth.

After nights of continuous struggles and days of mental deliberation, I had finally did it! I, Ganesha, the invisible one, had cracked the code! Not only did I now have an incredibly well-structured project that was making a ground-breaking program, but I had also experienced what sincerity and eventual accomplishment tasted like. I knew instantly that I wanted to test my parents' reactions and see how they felt about their son's work. With eager enthusiasm, I submitted my project and awaited results. While the expectation of bringing home good results to my parents and to see them being proud of me for my accomplishment was nerve-wrecking, I found myself to be experiencing something anew in this entire episode. I found my brain constantly thinking about my program, about the various logics I had applied to it and what more this could lead to if I delved deeper into coding. This seemed to have opened new avenues for me, got me into deeper understanding of the world of Computer Science and to think that almost every element of my imagination could be brought to life if I willed and worked.

While these little adventures went on inside my head, my father got a call from my college, asking both the parents to come to a meeting because of an 'alarming event'. This obviously did not sound good. I can recall that my parents had never taken me to be the most disciplined and studious boy, as far as boys of my age come, but I am sure they knew I was no major trouble maker. To be summoned thus was a reason for both shock and anger, but it had to be done and dealt with.

"Honestly, we thought we'd come home and have to ground Ganesha to put his life into order. But what happened at the college meeting was beyond our comprehension," recollects Parvati.

When my parents were brought into the principal's office, as they later told me, they found themselves in the audience of a strangely familiar man who they had seen on television. Was it that big?

"How bad could Ganesha have messed things up this time?" they wondered. But things changed drastically from the point they were greeted with a big smile and introduced to the Minister of Technology and Development. The meeting was actually held to talk about the incredulity of what I had built as a part of the academic project. The design of the program was built around graphic animation that converted imaginative world into real time 3D images and could help to generate visuals as per will, so to speak. With technical jargons thrown around in conversation, it was hard for the astounded couple to understand the nuanced level of their son's development. But from what the minister and the principal were saying, they fathomed that what their son had done was far from trouble. In fact, now they actually understood that I had possibly done something huge to attract such attention and appreciation. To think that their Ganesha, the happy-go-lucky boy who spent time in his own dream world or went hop-skip-jumping around with all sorts of people in the world, could actually build something so praiseworthy was no less than a miracle for them! The meeting wrapped up with promises of a conference and further exploration of the program, but in the essence, my parents were sent home with a grand token of appreciation and with a feeling of unbelievable pride that their son was a lot more than they had imagined him to be through all these years.

Talks begin and spread faster than wings, especially in small mountain towns where everybody knows each other. What I had started as a personal determination to build my own identity had been metamorphosed into a public discussion. However, like most conversations that happen amidst masses, there were more negative connotations to this than praise. From doubts to whether this was all actually just a rumour spread by my father by paying the authorities, to declarations that the project was actually a copy off the internet. Some 'well-wishers' even went on to say that I had just used one of Skanda's old practice books and tricked my way into fooling the teachers. It most certainly did not occur to anyone that this so called 'good for nothing' guy could also be a smart-brained programmer and build something. So the emergence of a simpleton as a programming genius roughed up some feathers; it's hard to say what happened more intently – the surprise and sarcasm of onlookers, as or the strengthening of my determination to walk up ahead on this path.

I practically have a mental picture etched in my memory from that evening, when my parents had walked into my room the instant they got home, actually sat down with me and asked me about the program, taken interest in the story I had to tell them about the newfound interest. They had even extended their congratulations, although I could tell it was awkward and almost unbelievable for them. However, amidst this confusion between relief and disappointment that I was nervously experiencing, was also a hint of enthusiasm about hope, accomplishment and above all, acknowledgement, albeit half-hearted, that my parents had extended by actually reaching out to me. This was clearly a first. Jumbo too looked up to stare at me a lot longer than usual, as though saying that he understood me, the deliberation and dilemma.

In the consecutive months, I completely submerged myself into the world of graphic interface. From conceptualization to visualization in 3D representations, there was no theory or language that I did not seek and understand. With the passage of time, I found myself discovering newer avenues, learning platforms and even online competitions that put me in the presence of coders, experts and computer programming enthusiasts from all over the world. From the hidden silence of my room, I had already begun making an online presence for myself strongly felt under the pseudonym of Jumbo, inspired from my rat and in sync with the spirit of my favourite animal, the reverential elephant, that is known for its wisdom, patience and benevolence all through the animal kingdom. Not only was this turning into a learning experience for me with opportunities that I could have never imagined, it was also turning out to be true that with growing sincerity and experience, I could steadily watch myself becoming somebody who people were recognizing for his skills and out of the box innovation in graphic programming. Not simply as Shiva and Parvati's son stumbling down the road.

It was around this time that my college invited me for a coding contest to be held in China. I was asked to represent them at the local level elimination round. The contest was based on development of a program that was unique and contributed to any solution for everyday use. The programmer with the least amount of development time would be declared the winner. Now, the challenge was that I came from a town where people studied hard, got placed in good engineering or management positions or became doctors. This is what my family had seen and believed in. The only idea of contest they understood was that of final examinations of graduation. While this invitation helped to establish their son's eligibility as a good coder, they did not think it was necessary for me to waste so much time on it, let alone the idea of going to another country to play a computer game, as they understood it. And hence, the initial response from them was a straight no. While the inherent obedience that I have been brought up with forbade me from arguing with my parents, the budding enthusiasm could not be silenced at this stage. This got me to secretly participate in the contest and thus began my series of post-dinner time preparations. With all the friends and beneficiaries I had earned through my years of 'frolicking around', I even managed to raise enough money to apply for my passport and other documents I would need might I clear the initial rounds of qualification. With time, my model got closer to its final stage. But I needed an endorser from the field of technology. After much deliberation, I turned to Skanda to recommend me for the final round. I prepped myself, pitched my idea, explained the secretive nature of the situation and extended a request in earnest. While Skanda was in awe with the concept and model that I was building for the contest and he had been very vocal about it, it was beyond his understanding to let this pass without our parents' knowledge. Despite my continuous pleadings, he ratted me out and I was hurled against the wrath of an angry father, the disdain of a disappointed mother.

Consequently, I was forced to withdraw from the competition and got back to my regular studies for the final examination of the final year of college. This was a challenging time for me, both emotionally and physically. Sometimes, I can still recall the helplessness and loneliness I used to feel locked up in my room. While the stress of passing my exams was imposed violently, the psychological thunder of betrayal was never let to die down. That was perhaps the first and only time I sat down and cursed myself, I can confess that now. I was thinking if I had made the biggest mistake of my life by opening this Pandora's box or whether I should get back into the comforts of shadows and invisibility. With efforts to forget everything I had learned and experienced in the past few months, I concentrated on being the average student, the satisfactory son and an acceptable person that I was always made out to be. It wasn't that the college corridors were not full of mocking laughs, neither were dinners devoid of doubtful glares for the boy. But amidst all this, the hopes of bringing my world of dreams to a three-dimensional reality stayed signed out from the real world with the name of Jumbo slowly gathering dust in the virtual world.

With the beginning of final exams, silence clouded the house. The only time anyone saw me was my walk to college and back between exams. Though I could sense that my mother's heart melted with love and concern for my well-being, a strong check was maintained to ensure no leniency was exercised as a bad influence. After an ordeal that went on for a month, I had finally written my last paper and had been assured that I would pass with good marks after post-exam assessment with my teachers. The glares of my parents eventually got milder, their words softer until one day, I was informed that I was being sent to my grandparents as a holiday gift. With a little relief and a lot of doubt, I left home to be away from everything I had built and learned and loved in the last year.

It was only after I was gone that one day, while cleaning up the room, mother found out my extensive research, the paperwork and concept that I had dedicated months to. She narrated the entire episode to me later. What she read and comprehended through the notes made her face turn pale. With tearful eyes, she took the concept note to father, who was left equally shocked and teary-eyed. They were spellbound with what I had done.

What was on that paper that had left my parents in shock and tears?

Was this redemption or blunder?

2
Know Thy Enemy

What did I last leave you with? Right, it was a mysterious revelation that my parents had had about me. While I had been sinking into the never-ending warp of doubts about my past, and more importantly, my future, things had been getting pretty intense back at home. When I had left to take a break from the hectic routine of academic grilling and emotional turmoil of home, I had hoped to leave behind all memories of my little virtual world that had come to a stand-still. Within the time span of a year, I had risen from the stature of being the ordinary shadow in an extraordinary family to finding my own passion, and frankly, I had fallen in love with this *avatar*. My imagination had gotten wings and fused with the use of technology to build a model of virtual reality. While I had found knowledge, recognition, excitement and appreciation, with these accreditations had come the curse of rejections, disappointments, rumours and pressure to return to normalcy as was the trend in the little town of Kailash. Battling through all of this, I gave up on the passion for 3D programming for virtual reality. In this storming oscillation of trying to find my footing, I had found the golden window to show to my parents what I was capable of doing, and more importantly, what they meant to me.

In the name of this contest of utility-based programing, I had built a model of virtual reality that would help to connect parents with their children across the world despite physical or geographical distances. I knew how much my parents missed Skanda, my elder sibling, ever since he had left for working in a respectable multinational organization as an engineer. I have to admit that I had my reservations against him, like most siblings do in the name of rivalry.

"Oh, Skanda, we miss you so much, the house feels so empty without you," Ma would always tell him dotingly.

I would be sitting right there, all seventy kilograms of me. (Yes, I have always been the healthier of the two siblings and heard no end of it!) Although stung by the attention and preference Skanda received from mom and dad, I could not overlook their grief and worry about him being so far away from home for the first time in his life. To my own surprise, I found myself feeling their pain and anxiety and became desperate to find a solution for this. The contest was an inspiration, honestly, but what really motivated me was this opportunity to get close to mom and dad, and to show them and the rest of the world that I was worth more than the family name. Now, I don't want to make this a boastful narrative of my character, but you have to know that I was sincere about my commitment. I had worked very hard and eventually, I came up with a dummy of the application that could help parents connect with their children and see them in their living situations, receive signals and notifications, sense emotions and deliver virtual hugs and messages through 3D holographic representations of each other. If this were to be developed full-fledged, it could turn into the biggest break-through in the science of virtual reality. Obviously, it needed a lot of development and improvement, but the concept and base model as it stood, was enough to place this development amidst the game changing technologies of the world. Unfortunately for me, and for the world, this idea had been nipped in the bud by my well-meaning parents who wanted me to focus on the conventional track, become a simple and stable professional and forget about experimentation.

"Darling, we only want what is best for you. Look at your brother, he is so intelligent and has made a stable career for himself," my father told me.

They had tried everything from affectionate discussions to aggressive instructions to divert me from my path. Quite frankly, I understood their fear. Our town was full of examples of people who could have made it large in life, but got distracted by attractions that brought them to dead end. And here I was, already being treated like a bad egg, simply because I had chosen to take a couple of steps to shine.

"Wrong steps," I thought back then. Apparently, this was a good sign. "Acceptance is the first step to success, son." Can you imagine my father in his stern voice, trying to be all soft and encouraging with me? I thought it was sort of cute!

So, like the loser I had always believed myself to be, I spent most part of my vacation with the grandparents trying to walk the line of conventions. It had been too late for me to sit for placements for the best companies because I had been too absorbed in completing my model. But there were still a couple of organizations which could help me save a face in front of the community and give my parents some relief. So I decided to sit for competitive exams that would get me into a stable job.

But what little mysteries fate had been laying down for my return to Kailash, I had no idea about! The world had turned upside down with the strange discovery that mom had made amidst the piles of research and notes I had left behind of my now discarded project.

"We were stunned by the concept note of what our son had been working on for nights. We had assumed and dismissed that phase as a computer addiction and an unnecessary risk in the path of his education," dad had confessed to the relatives in my absence. Mom, on the other hand, had been extremely overwhelmed, not only by 'creative expression of her son's skills and potential, but also spell bound by my love and concern for them. Again, her words, not mine, so please pardon my seemingly pompous tone. But I have to give it to them that despite not understanding the extent and exactness of the technical nuance of my model, they had at least figured out the sentiments behind it and felt proud. Things were about to change, and hopefully, for the better.

At the end of my vacations, I nervously returned to Kailash. I was all set to tell my folks that I had tried my best at the interviews and exams for placement at some of the preferred tech-based organizations of the country. It would be a little dishonest to say that I was personally excited about it. But I hoped that this would make it up to my parents for the disappointment they had felt in me. However, the atmosphere at home seemed oddly different.

Not only was I welcomed with an affection that surpassed mom's and dad's usually latent nature, but in the next few days, I found myself being attended to, spoken with and involved in almost everything that my parents were doing. My opinion was asked in matters of familial importance.

"Do you know our son has been declared the best coder of his college and even asked to represent the college in international competitions?" I heard dad boast to a friend one day. Can you imagine my confusion at what was going on? After being almost banished from the house to repent the diversion I had taken up, I was not only being welcomed back with arms wide open, but also being shown off to the community. For a moment, I even thought that I had stepped into one virtual reality, or this was just one crazy dream, just an alarm ring away from the gloomy reality!

On a fateful day, about a month after my return, I received a communication – an acceptance letter as a trainee engineer in a reputed organization. The first emotions I felt were not of joy or pride. It was relief. Finally, I had a documented proof that I was on the appropriate and acceptable track and hopefully, my parents would hold me in at least some regard as compared to Skanda, the apple of their eye. Despite the inner turmoil and surrender I felt about the final lock shut on my passion, I was coming to understand what being an adult meant in this world. For the first time, I felt that coming out of the shadows of my privileges also meant giving up on my comfort zone, doing things that I did not necessarily agree with and perhaps to think beyond myself. Too heavy to be coming from the mind of a teenager? Perhaps, yes. But the kind of drama my life was driving me around in also called for dramatic thoughts, you see; so I am only playing my part! Little did I know, however, that there was another script being written behind my back.

When I took the letter of acceptance to my parents, I didn't quite get the response I had anticipated. Not that they didn't smile and congratulate me on my accomplishment.

"Oh, wow! You did it boy. We always knew you had it in you," they said it bleakly like I had told them I wanted to have curry rice for dinner. I could tell that something was amiss. "It is so difficult to understand parents," I was thinking, "I don't know what it is that I have to do to get them to be happy and content with me, just as they are with Skanda!" Back then, I had no idea that what I believed to be 'amiss' in the eyes of mom and dad was really the love and realization that they wanted to express, and to revert his pursuit pack to his passion.

"Son, you make us proud, no doubt about that. But more than that, you humble us with your love and sacrifice," dad declared dramatically. It was then that the overwhelmed couple revealed to me what they had found out about my project. Everything made sense now. The change in attitude, the sudden show of support and almost miraculous public display of affection now fell into line with the revelation.

With the emotions and expectations resolved between the family members, dad told me, in one of his one on one conversations, that I was not to feel any pressure to join the job I had been offered at their account. "I want you to know that I have complete faith in you and no matter what you chose to do up ahead from here, I am going to be there for you," he said warming up to me. At this stage, the idea really presented itself to me, that what my parents were really hinting at was that I could choose to follow the set path of professional jobs or I could actually make my own path, based on the developments I had made so far. Were they really suggesting I could start something of my own? I had to pinch myself a few times and even bring up different versions of this idea with my parents to assess if I had understood them correctly. Turns out, I had! So, in lieu of the recent developments, my head started tilting towards the idea of starting my own venture. But as teaching lessons is life's favorite sport, I still had a lot of game to play and lose, before I could taste victory.

I wish I could say that hearing my parents praise my passion or even extending their unconditional support was all the magic I needed to make up my mind. Back then, at the beginning of my career graph, it felt like a huge responsibility to make a decision based on half known facts, and honestly, the lack of experience. Now, for all the aspiring beginners in the world of technology, or even enterprise in general, I want to send out a disclaimer message. While the idea of breaking away from the norm, being your own boss and embarking an entrepreneurial journey sounds exciting and looks all shiny, you have to look beyond the glamour of these phrases. There's a lot to be considered before you jump to being an entrepreneur. Again, just to clarify, this doesn't mean you shouldn't follow your heart and pursue your dreams, but this has to be done with a degree of responsibility and deliberation. I know I went through a lot of that! The dilemma was this – following the conventional path of a secured engineering job would be comfortable and safe. There would be a future, there would be a set path to follow, and above all, there would be a psychological and financial stability as long as the work was done rightly and religiously. That alone is more than one can aspire for. On the other hand, working with these organizations, especially in the kind of profile I would be entering, would undermine my potential and put me many paces behind on my learning curve (again, I know I am bordering at sounding arrogant or over confident. But let's face it, guys, if I didn't make something out of the determination and support life had given me, you'd call me a waste!). If I started something of my own, I could work on my own terms, actualize the product I had been building all this while, and very importantly, all of my hard-work could be focused. On the other hand, to continue on this path would involve a lot of risks, barely any precedence to follow and no financial guarantee. At the crossroads of this vital decision, I was encouraged by the words of my father to analyze all the possibilities.

"The best way to face your enemy (or challenge in this case) is to know your dueler inside out. Once you have done that, you will not have unforeseen surprises, unplanned escalations or any reservations about what you're getting into."

I think that was an important piece of advice. Not only did it bring a much-needed insight, but also gave me a link to start with. Anyone who has begun something of their own would nod vehemently reading this that often the dilemma is about the starting point.

Thus began my quest to "know thy enemy". One of the first things that happened was the making of lists. I had a list for the people I wanted to talk to, a list of articles I had to read, a list of things I knew, a list of things I didn't know. I even had a list of things I would need. (This included pens and papers and popcorns too!). Yes, I am a man of details. This was my homework phase and I wanted to do it well. So I dived in and started bringing out pieces of gems that I felt would come in handy. I remember noting that my father often came into my room (which had now become my space for work and brain storming). I think a part of me was happy, and a part eager to please. I thought the more information I brought and pinned to my board, the more impressive my preparation would be (and look too!).

A couple of months into this research mode, I was sitting with my parents and they were causally chit-chatting with me about the progress, and I was explaining, almost impressed with myself about all the things I knew. And then, just like that, my mother placed a simple question before me, "So, what is this enterprise going to be?" You will not believe the number of deep breaths I had to take to calm my racing brain. I did not have an answer! I had been so busy collecting information that I had completely gotten lost about what I had begun with. "That, my son, is why you need to make a goal-post and then decide which players and moves you will need to score the goal." Now, I have known that my mother has sometimes been forced to watch football with me, but to hear her quote this example at me was another level of surprise, and one so accurate too! In that moment, I realized that a bullish approach to hard-work would only exhaust me. I need to pull out a focus and then dedicate a directed approach. Consequently, I began the process of narrowing down what I really wanted my enterprise to be. I made a final list of things of yes and no – about the things that could work as a business and things that couldn't. In the bigger picture of technological development, I found my focus to be on virtual reality, with my focus on development of applications that would enable mobility in one form of another. This at least appeared as a convincing enough point to start with. Henceforth, I revised my research on the basis of knowledge, current scenario in the tech-space, both at the national and international levels, relevant resources required for implementation, business opportunities and challenges that would come my way in the next steps.

It was around this time that I started talking to people – developers, corporate and funders – to understand the current situation and to scout for people who may be most effective and efficient partners for me. Within the first month of stepping into the precarious waters of this advent, I had already begun to realize that this would not be as easy as it had appeared back in the days of feverish coding through the nights. While the plan of action, requirements and expectations were all beautifully chalked out on my dashboard, I was yet to take the first risky steps into the world of entrepreneurship. In the coming times, there were many lessons I would learn and many hardships I would face.

Continue into the next chapter to know more about my journey.

3
Building a Foundation

There is a reason why more than half of the people in this world are working for others. It is not because they don't have ideas of their own, it's not that they don't want to become their own bosses and work on converting their own dreams into reality. It's not even that they may not be able to arrange the appropriate set of resources, financial or otherwise, if they really got their hands on things. The problem really arises in stepping out of the comfort zone, knowingly giving up the state of a stable and secured financial and emotional (sometimes, even social stability). That's where the real border between dreams and reality comes alive. And frankly, this is where most people say, 'ah, forget it, I am happy in my comfortable world'.

Honestly, Kailash has always been the comfortable home for me. I was born here, fought with my father here, even raged many battles through childhood and adolescence here. Ever since I was young, every single person in Kailash has known me; many even worship me for the kind of things I have pulled off, despite being seen as a rather fat and carefree kid. Honestly,

I have sort of become used to this treatment, of being Shiva and Parvati's son, in being known and respected by the people of my life. You can imagine, it would take a huge step out of my comfort zone to start something from scratch, something my folks will take a lot of time to understand, let alone approve. It is one thing to sit in my assuring room and consult with the various constellations and stars to give me an idea of how I am doing, whether my timing is right and if the road I have chosen will be a lucrative one. But to delve into an affair with other humans, to test my theoretical designs, and to assess their reactions to my creation is another ball-game altogether.

Now, I have to admit, as Ganesha, few things have come to me as a privilege that I know many others would not have received. Forget about all the endless support I received from my parents (and I will continue to reiterate that time and again), I practically had access to any information I wanted. My point being, that I had the luxury of availing the best resources of knowledge from Uncle Brahma, free internet libraries from the constellations (Mount Kailash has the best Wi-Fi in the entire universe, you see…) so that I could make the best of my time in researching about the virtual reality (VR) technology, and as far as doing my homework on VR was concerned, I was set.

If you're a young member of an average Indian family and if you are treading anywhere off from the path of following what is expected of you, you should know that people around you would test your motivation and confidence and with all their might, try to find a flaw in your logic, irrespective of whether you want to be a singer, a universe maker, a cinematographer or a hapless entrepreneur like me! Imagine my father leaving his Deconstruction business, or my Uncle Brahma taking off from his Creative Agency. Or what if Nandi Kaka, our beloved caretaker stopped doing all the unimaginable things for us that makes our life run so smoothly! Nobody would go tell them to 'follow your dreams, the rest will follow', you know?

As expected, this is what happened in my world of relatives and family friends too.

"So, Ganesha, have you really tried your hand at all the interviews for campus placements? Did nothing work out?" came the first 'well-meant' question during my first social gathering at Lakshmi Aunty's 6000th birthday party.

"You know, maybe you should start small, with the Mansarovar Lake; my son knows a lot of contractors there who help remove obstacles. They will certainly hire you." I was beginning to realize the concept of willingly not taking up my job had still not been understood by most of my relatives. Their good intentions and concerns were showered liberally as I tried to explain my desire to start something of my own in the field of Virtual Reality.

I would say to them, "You see uncle, the universe you see today is only accessible physically. If the people down below Kailash want to speak to us, they will have to cross over, so they can personally meet us. Or imagine, now that Skanda has gone away to the lowlands of earth, if mother Parvati has to meet him, she will have to walk down there to give him handmade food, right?" I thought I had simplified it to the basics, "So I want to create a system where it will be possible to access this reality more easily." The reply outsmarted me by miles, not quite what I had imagined.

"So you want to open your own parallel universe? Maybe you should work for some time at your Brahma Uncle's store;

you would learn a lot about business, see how it works," said Narada Chacha. Now, I am not saying that any of these advices were meant as derogation or even meant to confuse me, but unfortunately, they ended up making me avoid such social encounters with people who were dying to tell me what to do! What made it worse was that people who had no idea even about reality development, let alone virtual reality, were trying to instruct me about the next course of action. Don't get me wrong, I do not mean this as an insult to their intelligence or intentions. But there's something about new-age startups and even VR that everybody does not know or understand. Somewhere amidst all that chaos, I started feeling the urgent need to meet people who were in sync with my idea and understanding who would be able to give me a lucrative perspective. Unfortunately, in Kailash, there was no one who could match this requirement.

Have you heard them say that necessity is the mother of all inventions? It's true in the celestial world too! I did what anyone in my position would do. I turned to my own powers to find a solution. I decided I would invent my own set of companions who would be able to be my alter-egos, my friends and guides, if you will. These 'friends' would help me get an objective perspective and perhaps be onboard for brainstorming. Thus, with the help of Ma Parvati, who is an expert in breathing life into things, I designed two aspects of my own personality into real life persons.

I turned to the only available social circle I had left in the city. "I see two sides of you, son, the one I love and the one that the world loves. They are both going to be your friends and bring out the best in you," she prophesied generously.

My first friend was Chintan; he had a logical mind, believed in rational, well-planned decisions and reflected the deep thinker in me. He was older than me by a few years and held the maturity that one needs to make critical decisions in life. The other 'friend' that became the manifestation of the other half of my personality was Srijan. The creative one, just a few years younger than me; he was bright spirited, impulsive, energetic and extremely intuitive. He brought the art and harmony into the equation. Thus, with the three of us, it became an equation of balance, diversity and perfection. In my head, this marked the beginning of the thinking phase – the backstage part of the game.

Some of the first discussions that came to the table were about the arena of VR that I could build on as a product for the trending services. "You know, real estate is doing extremely well these days, but what it really lacks is a make-belief influence that can get the target audience to really imagine their property before the purchase," my friend Chintan offered his two-pence. My other friend Srijan, on the other hand, who was a gamer to the heart and was up-to date with the latest trends in the young generation, had a different opinion. "If you want to enter the tech space, you have to appeal to the young mass, not with property, but with interactive media, maybe even gaming!"

I think you get an idea of what most of these conversations would have been like. There were discussions, propositions, rejections and assimilations. At that stage, it felt to me like the perfect process. The three of us seemed to make an effective combination with our individual sense of subject knowledge, market analysis and creative understanding. Putting all permutations to logic, we eventually came to the conclusion that there were four logical avenues that could be explored with VR. These could be real estate, gaming and multimedia, food and travel industry. It was settled then. Or it seemed back then. But I was soon to realize that this was only the beginning of the new phase of struggles for me. My new series of homework began with researching about each of these sectors to see how best VR would fit into the scenario. I have to admit though that the more I read, the more enchanted I got with each of these wings. It seemed that an unending loop was forming between research and decision-making. The more I read, the more attracted I got to each of the idea, and the more difficult it got for me to pick any one idea, the more I continued researching about all of them!

It was during these times of indecision that one day Srijan came to me with the information that a new intra-galaxy travel agency was opening up in Kailash, one of Vishnu Uncle's associates in-fact, had decided to set-up easy transportation between mortal world and Kailash, making Mansarovar Lake accessible like never before! Now, it is a known fact that every year, Kailash witnesses a huge footfall as religious tourism, but it is also true that there is no real organized and advanced facility to make a good business out of this phenomenon. This news of a new travel agency brought in itself an opportunity for us to collaborate and bring about a VR model that could integrate with and enhance the entire experience. It was in that quick 'light bulb' moment that my mind was made up about basing my enterprise on tourism, starting with a product catering to my own mountain and other religious and adventurous avenues around it. It all seemed probable back then. Thus, the idea began.

I remember Uncle Vishnu had told me once, "The building of an enterprise is based on many pillars – a product, a revenue model, a team, funds, etc." This at least gave me some flag marks to start with. On my way ahead, I learned that there are many more. As far as my next steps were concerned, I was going by the check list. I had the blueprints of my product in mind. It would be a virtual-interactive model of the religious sites that people actually came to Kailash for. In my opinion, backed by the opinion of my friends who were now turning into my business partners, we would be able to attract a lot of crowd by helping them visualize what their destinations would really look like. It was based on a simulator mechanism that would attract potential travellers. All we had to do was strike deals with travel agencies to integrate our product into their marketing schemes.

"This would be a good entry point for us, you know. We should start small and once the model starts proving itself on the ground, we will diversify into other geography too," Chintan had suggested with what sounded like absolute conviction and farsightedness. The revenue model was simple. It was a simple portal that would bring real life experiences to the potential travellers and convert enquiry into sales for the travel agency. We would license our product out for a yearly subscription plan based on the number of potential uses. The team consisted of the three of us, with our respective intelligence and experience, which did not seem all that much, but would collectively amount to making an all-rounder system. We realized we were not in the position of seeking investors until we had footed ourselves at the ground level and decided to seek aid from our friends and family members. It would have had to be a humble beginning. I remembered Lakshmi Aunty having kindly offered to support me during one of our conversations and thus I turned to her for help. "I will give you just a little to start off with, Ganesha," she explained, "not because I don't trust you, but simply because it will teach you how to keep your feet grounded."

We worked out of my house, only spending the bare-minimum necessary on the most basic hardware and software required. We thought we'd improvise and build on from square one. Honestly, I had been opposed to this idea. "But we should save as much capital as possible; we will need a lot of it later. Besides, if you start spending on one thing, next thing you know, you will start spending on everything!" Chintan would object at the slightest hint of new expenditures. It was like having a very strict accountant on-board. It felt like a good thing to keep us in check.

Once our basic infrastructure was in place, we delved diligently into product building. Since there weren't many prototypes to fall back on, we were heavily reliant on theories and our own innovation. We split our responsibilities. While I focused my attention on the technological development of the program, Srijan, the Creative Director, began designing the front end of the VR experience of Kailash; it was his job to bring about the appearance of the geography into the program. Chintan, with his background and orientation took on the business side of the enterprise, coming up with financial and marketing strategy once the model was ready. I have to admit that back then, this seemed like a pretty intense phase. We were actually very proud of all the work we were doing and the world we were building from within the four walls of my room.

After a period of about six months, our product was ready to be introduced to the real world. I had built the program to be viewed as a pair of glasses that looked into a VR box. This box would create the audio-visual effects of a very believable experience of a tour in and around Kailash, depending on the kind of view any viewer wanted to see or the travel agency wanted to pitch. Srijan had actually gone into these locations and collected the visuals and incorporated this experience into my codes. Chintan, on the other hand, had built our very first presentation, came up with our entire financial flow-chart to pitch to potential clients. With a vision to start a revolution with our breakthrough innovation, Chintan, Srijan and I came up with the name of our enterprise. We would be called Shrishti – a vision of the creation. While it had a religious tone to it that would appeal to our target audience for religious tourism, it also portrayed a life-like impression that was the ultimate intension of our product. It did feel like handling my own universe from within the VR controller. I could feel how my uncles and fathers felt going about their everyday affairs!

"We should do something extraordinary for the launch," Srijan exclaimed in his usually excited tone! You can imagine Chintan's immediate recoiling with the calculation of expenses, "We are a startup, we can't afford that kind of luxury! Let's keep it simple."

But I knew we needed a big start to attract attention. We sent out customized star-studded invitations to all the special gods, from both, Heaven as well as underground. We even made a live webcast across galaxies and telecast for earth for people travelling to different worlds. Goddess Saraswati, who is known across the universe for her wisdom and knowledge, happens to be very good friends with my mother. And I pulled some strings to have her on-board as the chief guest for the inauguration. There was no doubt that wherever she went, a stream of inter-galactic media, headed by Narada himself, would follow.

The launch was a huge success; huge not only by the parameters of an event in Kailash, but with live webcast and contributing participants from all over the country, we did make a huge impact in the online world, with a visibility in various demographics. Srijan had arranged for meteor showers and Chintan made an excellent constellation presentation in the night sky that stopped time for everybody!

As beginners, this was enough to motivate us; we had won the hearts of people for various reasons. We were showing the glory of their beloved Kailash which appealed to them with a sense of pride. For the elders, it was a miracle; for the youngsters, it had a modern appeal; for businessmen, well it was perhaps seeding their own imagination as to what this technology would do in their respective fields. We received acknowledgement from the After-life Tourism Association and they congratulated us on the idea. A lot many introductions were made and appointments arranged to discuss details. All these were really good signs.

At the end of the day, we felt like little children who had been playing with sand castles all this while and had been gifted a real-life castle to own! "I think we deserve to dine like kings, just for tonight!" I remember Chintan's face as he made this generous proposition that evening. Srijan and I had just exchanged shocked looks. I guess a taste of what success may feel like gives everyone a kick. In my head, I could replay the span of struggle that I had encountered, from harnessing my skills to convincing my parents, from stepping way out of my comfort zone to slowly building an idea from scratch to an actual, physical product that I could show people as a proof of all my hard work. I had finally come out of the shadows I had been fighting against and now, I could move ahead with a concrete accomplishment in my hand. While my spirits were soaring in the sky, my feet were rooted in the ground as I was completely aware of the responsibilities that lay ahead of me. My loving parents had battled judging neighbours to stand by their son's decisions and I knew that I had to step forward, mindful of all these sacrifices.

In that moment of deep introspection, I felt that I had made the wise decision of really doing my homework and preparing well about my venture. I knew every nut and bolt of VR now and could use its application realistically in the tourism industry and create a revolution. I knew that it was because of my backstage efforts and research that I could confidently stand on the stage and speak to people with confidence. More than anything else, I knew it was this understanding that would take me miles ahead in my game as my founding steps into the world of enterprise.

Lesson – Mount Kailash stands tall and strong through millenniums of existence and storms, not because of how nicely it shines under the moonlight, but because of its strong and thick base.

It is the strength of your knowledge that helps to set the foundation of your endeavours. When it comes to doing your homework, there's no end to how much is enough. While your eyes are set on the final result, it helps to have your head grounded with the depth of understanding of your subject; only that will help you rise high to the peak of your success!

4

The Glimmer and Darkness

$\mathcal{I}$ t is said that the stars play a very important role in determining what happens in life of the mortals. If the constellations are in your favour, you can ace the race despite all the mistakes and challenges you encounter in your journey. On the other hand, if stars disagree with you, they have their own way of showing you their power. Some say that humans have a way of 'changing their stars', but I wonder how it works up here for us. We may be able to control the stars, but contrary to mortal belief, even we are not 100% insured against failures or mishaps. My own experience is that you need to keep working towards what you believe is perfection and be welcoming towards success and failures equally because if one brings pride, the other offers humility – both of which are essential ingredients to the path of accomplishments. Believe it or not, the divine has a much deeper plot in creating failures than it does in designing success!

Apparently, the constellations have been playing around with me even without my own knowledge. Especially around the time when Shrishti – my first venture into Virtual Reality – had just begun taking its first steps. Right after the launch, Srijan, Chintan and I started out with a very aggressive approach towards creating inter-galactic awareness about the product.

"There is no dearth of creative gods with power, Ganesha! While Brahma has much better contacts than you, I am also worried about Yamraj who has been known for being the leader in the travel industry, especially from earth to divine lands," Chintan brought up his concern on one of those days when we were strategizing about our next moves. Our launch had been a huge success and we had had enquiries coming in. But Chintan was right; it wouldn't take very long for people to understand and replicate our concept, especially for those who had a better hold in the industry and were in a better position to influence the fraternity. As you know, most gods up here are related to one another and loyalties are stronger than you would imagine on earth!

"We are racing against time, and our focus right now should be to create an edge over anyone else, to penetrate the market so aggressively with our uniqueness that nobody stands a chance," Srijan was already thinking of creative campaigns in his head, I could tell as he spoke enthusiastically.

Once again, with a meticulous alignment of our expertise between creativity, business skills and technical knowledge expertise, we dived into creating a brand image that would resonate across the universe. Our individual domains were all focused into Shrishti's advertisement, even as a little, small-time business started trickling into our little office at Kailash. Our very first client was from a small town in Nepal, where a group of elderly men and women were contemplating to visit Kailash for Shivratri, but were apprehensive about the facilities available to make their visit comfortable. This travel agency, that ran by the name of Garuda Travels, wanted to sell the trip of Kailash as comfortable and serene. It was our job to create a VR graphic to let them experience this journey, keeping in mind the attractions that these elderly could relate with.

"See, this is exactly what our USP is! We can customize and cater to specific demands of people, that makes us desirable to your needs, no matter what it is!" Chintan was getting more and more aggressive about pitching us as a customer specific product. And it seemed to be working.

"That is what brought me to your organization; your telecasts on social media have been creating a buzz," Garuda spoke over web conference. It was obvious then that our word had been spreading across different platforms. "This is where our focus should be," we unanimously decided, perhaps that's when marketing became our official mantra.

It is one thing to make a decision and another to break it down to the nitty-gritty of how, when, why and what. Several brainstorming sessions began occupying our days. Most of our times would be split between research, deliberation and development – the three arenas split amidst the three of us. Days spilled into nights and weekdays stole into weekends; this had become our endless loop of trial and error for coming up with the best marketing strategies. Unfortunately, this was all that we were being able to do! Honestly, I wouldn't have even noticed we were running short of man-power until mother Parvati bellowed at me one day.

"You're drowning yourself with this bullish labour without taking care of yourself or your partners. How far do you think you'd be able to push with this attitude?" She had lost her temper after reminding us for the hundredth time to come home for dinner. But in that one moment of being shaken up to reality (and even though it had been with reference to our eating habits), it rang a bell of truth. "Your mother is right, Ganesha," Srijan suggested, "This won't do."

"But we can't afford getting more people on board with the budget constrains," chanted Chintan for the hundredth time.

That night, at the dinner table, after discussions with mother and father, Chintan and Srijan, and dear Uncle Nandi, two major decisions were made. First, we were going to hire interns to help distribute tasks. Second, we were going to seek funding to be able to work more diligently on our marketing strategies. "It is a happy feeling to have decisions made. They give you a roadmap for the next steps." If it were only that simple...

Who are the people that are available readily, will work diligently and quietly and are so flexible that they can practically get in and out of any situation? "Why did I not think of this before," thought I. My dearest helpers and supporters, my friends in need, my entire rally of rats! See, when you're a startup, just kicking into your business, there are many risks you will need to take, and many unplanned expenses too. You may or may not be ready for some of these imperatives, but things have to be done. Thus, to ensure compensatory actions and efficiency in terms of both capital and human resources, hiring interns is a prevalently effective trend. They may come with less experience, but with the right choice, you can find yourself a team of knowledgeable, sincere and hard-working bunch of youngsters who are eager to learn and willing to go the extra mile at the starting of their career. "Just make sure you don't have me baby-sitting them the whole time," Chintan never took efforts to hide his concerns. And I knew it was critical to get them on-board as help and not as liability.

It is here that I'd like to point out how extremely important your family can be when you are venturing out on your own. I have heard a lot of people, especially humans, complain and distance themselves from family when it comes to business. Maybe it's the fear of judgment, or the pressure of living up to their expectations or perhaps a trust issue; but most entrepreneurs don't mingle business with personal relations. I, on the other hand, have had a very different experience. Everybody knows that my father is known for his anger, and my mother for her vigorous strength and discipline. You can imagine the kind of pressure it could have on me to indulge their involvement with my enterprise. But I am not lying when I tell you that this has been the best decision. Not only do they criticize and question me on critical decisions and latest developments, but also provide best available support when necessary. I say this now because when we decided to hire the rat squad as interns, it was my father who immediately proposed asking Nandi Uncle to lend his managerial services to us, to manage and guide the team while we focused our attention on the more important issues.

"But father, isn't Nandi Uncle working with you already and won't your work get affected if he moves with us?" I was overwhelmed with his kindness and yet concerned for his sake.

"I have many others to support me, son," he declared. "Besides, decentralization of tasks is what empowers other members of your team to increase their capacity. Always remember that." In that one sentence, he had given me a very precious asset and a very precious advice, both.

The next few days were spent brainstorming on the investment strategy and how to approach funding agencies for the humongous marketing budget we had drafted. It felt prodigious, but we thought it would be best for our brand image and advertising. Chintan and I sat for hours preparing our pitch for this purpose. "It should be flashy, like we are selling the next big thing in the industry. And we need to make it as life-like as possible, let them feel what we do!" was his idea of creating an impression. I couldn't agree more. Thus, with all our time, a considerable share of the little business we had begun to make, and some interns put to design the interface, we were ready with our pitching presentation. We would be able to use this with several agencies with basic customization and would most likely create a good impression.

It was then that we met my Aunt Lakshmi who is known to have funded many startups. She was responsible for the mighty Dev-Lok empire – a housing estate for many gods. She also funded the construction of several planets and the availability of natural resources. When mother threw in a good word on our behalf, Aunt Lakshmi pulled some strings and got us an appointment with Kuber, the owner of the most reputed and powerful funding agency in the Universe. It is said that without his advice, no other agency will even rattle a coin in their pockets. "I can't fund you right now, since you are just starting out and

I generally invest only at the expansion phase with Series A or Series B funding, it won't be appropriate. Kuber, on the other hand, is well-known for his angel funding… he will help with the seed fund if you manage to impress him." Seed funding, as Aunt Lakshmi had explained, was like the kick-start investment people made in your business if they were impressed with your business model and were willing to put faith in your venture at an early stage; those who invest in early stage ventures are literally called angels! It was a big deal to have secured a personal meeting with Kuber, who was a prestigious business angel, and I was not going to leave any thread unstitched to win his confidence.

When I met him, I expected a long interrogation, a grilling session about all the financial plans, revenue model and product growth. I had prepared myself endlessly with answers that may pop up. But in that very meeting, within the first five minutes in front of Mr. Kuber, I learned what makes the world go around, what makes stars shine endlessly and what alchemy works behind making money out of nothing. "Why do you want to do this?" The first and only question Kuber asked me.

The world danced around my eyes, the desperation to prove myself, the hard-work I had put in the set up the prototypes, the taste of success at the launch, the rush of setting up an enterprise, the charm of what virtual reality can do, the way every moment spent on Shrishti makes me feel… all these emotions rushed into my head. "Because this is my dream, my reality and my passion," said I, surprised at how strong and real it felt to the bones. I don't know what he saw in that sentence. If emotions drove him to actions, or if that's how old and wise people function, but we got our first round of funding. This marked a new beginning. With the luxury of monetary liberties, our plan for selling Shrishti as a top brand started working towards reality.

The next few months were chalked out to design the best brand campaign of Shrishti. We split our work in a way to distribute tasks through the day. Chintan once again took to determining the cost distribution and marketing strategies of the campaign. He had been allotted a team of rats to do the running around for market research, lead generations and for securing the most prominent dates of planetary movements for airing our advertisements. Srijan and his team of creative rodents got down to working on the content for different platforms of media. They had plans designed for sky-cast, for print media across most divine galaxies and even for dream telecasts for mortals. I was behind that idea. My job, every single day, was to understand and assess the marketing and creative needs of the colleagues and complement that with VR, whether it was designing low-cost personalized marketing equipment or simply integrate the creative visualization into the interface. The first hour of my day was spent answering queries over emails and for making calls with the potential clients with reference to new orders. The rest of my mornings were dedicated to sitting with the entire Shrishti fleet, looking at updates and the plan for the rest of the day. I spent a religious amount of time in connecting with the stalwarts of the travel industry sharing our latest products are advertisements, mostly to gauge their response, but also to make sure that we registered a strong brand recall value for them.

I have to admit though that through all of this, I had a nagging thought at the back of my head that I was getting distracted, more like forgetting something very important I needed to focus on at that stage. But with funder meetings lined up, I couldn't afford distractions, hence this thought, like an alarm on snooze, was forgotten under layers of anxiety. Here's another lesson for you. When you're beginning to work on something, a business or any idea, you will often find yourself anxious about things. You will question the direction you are taking or simple decisions you are making. It is important here to remove yourself from your personal position and evaluate these doubts. While I don't recommend that you take every hint of anxiety and convert it into serious self-doubts, but you should definitely flag some repeated enquiries that you maybe subconsciously making about your decisions. I know this because I didn't do it.

Our advertisements slowly started capturing and dominating most of the media networks. Suddenly our visibility shot up massively across galaxies. Humans started sharing their thoughts about us; Shrishti started trending on social media and a much planned series of PR investments got us featured in the most widely read publications across the three Loks. Everyone knew us now; everyone spoke about us too. The number of enquiries, visits of clients and potential funders shot up dramatically. Chintan, Srijan and I were convinced that we had aced our very first strategy and had already half won the race!

With the aggressively strategized phase of marketing done to its deal, it was now time to reap the benefits and start working on the business coming our way. With the shift in focus, our work methodology would have to change too. "You should sit with the interns and let them ask questions…" Uncle Nandi had pointed out one day, "Not only will it be good for an over-all learning, but this will also help to throw light on issues you may not have noticed or miscalculated." I mulled over this thought for a while and finally decided to hold an all hands question-answer session every week.

"This might be a waste of our time, Ganesha," Chintan had reasoned. "We are at our peak after the campaign and I don't think we can afford this distraction."

But I respected Nandi Uncle's insight and Srijan backed me up, "I agree that a third person's perspective and question might help us with more innovation."

A couple of months later, on the day of an all-hands meetings, when I came into the office, I asked one of the interns to prepare a list of the business enquiries we had received in the past week and asked him to assess Shrishti's needs on the basis of the current trend. I had just received a call from Narada. "You're a hit, Ganesha!" he had exclaimed, "Everybody in the Dev Lok is talking about Shrishti now." I thanked him for the feedback and walked gloating into the meeting hall. I had no idea that what happened inside that room would change my perspective and confidence.

"Why is it that the number of queries seems to have shot tremendously but our conversion rate is as low as 2%? What has been our return of investment from the Series A funding? Sir, why are none of clients returning after the first pitch, or sometimes after piloting our prototype?" I couldn't take the questions of my interns anymore. In the race to have our name shine the brightest in the galaxy, we had completely sidelined the actual work that needed to shine brighter than the name. We had been spending endlessly on the marketing campaign to attract customers, but once these customers had our attention, we fell flat on their expectations in terms of our product value.

"Sir, there's an email that says we are like a fancy shop with stale sweets," an intern pointed out quoting an old Hindi phrase that had been slapped on us from one of our Indian clients. I knew I had slipped. Remember that nagging thought at the back of my head? I now knew what it was about. I had forgotten what Shrishti was really all about and had been blown away with all the excitement, race and glamour of fame. Rightly so, I had been put back to my place by the more simplistic, basic and critical perspective that the innocent interns had not yet forgotten. Having spent a great deal of our funds in marketing, aping what the big brands do had felt right at one stage, but in hindsight, it had wiped off our core value, the strength of our expertise and blinded us into a distracted path. It didn't take us long to realize that like a huge explosion, this marketing fool-hardiness had created a lot of noise, but left behind a black hole in our efforts.

Moral – *Through the journey of an enterprise, there will be many attractive paths to take. Some will shine bright with their glamour, some will look like the shortest, easiest paths. Building an enterprise is like walking at the edge of a sword. The key is balance. Curtail your expenditures and you will not grow, over-spend and you will find yourself in an expensive, sinking ship. But it is important to set our focus from a point and then dive nose-deep avoiding all attractions and distractions. The way you distribute your funds should be a result of far-sighted planning and not impulsive decisions. There will be many moments during business management, when things will seem rational and appealing, but these are the moments when you need to pause, inspect and then choose your roads.*

5

Understanding Business
and its Failure

Y
ou know what the problem with the Lord Sun is? He is too bright. In his training period, Sun had learned that in order to be seen, you need to shine above all others. It is important to do that to fill up all the darkness, to provide the necessary directions that others can follow and to make sure that you are seen with all your strength and potential. But as Lord Sun grew further into his career, he became more and more obsessed with shining and less focused on why he needed to shine, or how much! In this process, he started burning up all the resources he had at a magnanimous rate, "the brighter, the better, after all!" thought he. Soon, he became the brightest god in the galaxy, bright enough for everyone to see, even from other galaxies. Everybody started talking about him and stories were written on how bright he was. However, there came a time when he got too bright; so bright that people started averting his gaze and started keeping at a distance. Initially he thought maybe they were jealous of him.

But soon he realized that he was burning up people who tried to come close to him. The worst part was that in the process, he was also harming himself; almost burning himself inside out. In the rush to burn too bright, he had completely lost track of what he needed the brightness for and ended up distancing himself from everyone. That was Sun God's problem. I had grown up with Mother Parvati narrating his stories to me, with little morals to follow, to never be arrogant, to find my focus and to keep my well-wishers close by. As a kid, these had seemed like interesting stories. I would imagine Sun God with a big mouth, eating his own parts and thinking someone would have to be really dim to not realize how much harm they were causing for themselves. Up until the time I started doing it myself...

After having secured the seed funding from Kuber, we had been on cloud nine. With the luxury of money, all our limitations had been broken down and expenses shot up. Drowned with the bling of marketing and with the hope of speeding up the popularity of Shrishti, we had been blinded. The result had been catastrophic. Not only had we completely lost focus from our product and business development, but also managed to spend an embarrassingly major portion of our funding on building and lighting up a castle whose foundation had not been strengthened yet. It wasn't until our interns had been put to task for evaluation raised questions about our investment value and customer base attracts our attention.

The launch had been a huge success, the media and marketing strategies had been working fine, creating the buzz we expected them to. After all, a lot had been spent into making the noise! However, if asked about any business that we may have acquired, let alone aced, we had none to speak of. As our interns in the business development arena had pointed out, the buzz had led to several inquiries because everybody wanted to find out what the bling was all about. Uncle Narada had given us a short report about the media reach and the results had been very satisfactory. The Dev Lok had been talking about VR like it was the next big thing.

"We can explore VR for reaching out to humans in case they don't get our messages through dreams or nature," Varun, the god of wind had suggested.

"It even makes avatars a lot easier now! Imagine the kind of travel we had to do every time a sage prayed too hard or someone innocent got into trouble!" exclaimed an excited Chandra Dev.

Elsewhere in the galaxy, people on earth had been talking about life like their dreams have become, Narada's report explained. Even for the *Rakshasas* (demons) in the *Atala* (the underground world of demons), this model of VR seemed to be attracting a lot of attention to save the trouble of scaring people in person. A quick glance at this report seemed like a sign that we were headed in the right direction. Good ego-massage. We were making virtual reality more popular than even the most popular reality television shows on earth! But with popularity came a lot of noise, and yet no business. The worst part was that we were all out of funds now to sustain the expenses we had begun incurring at an exponential level. All the efforts in creating a brand with extensive advertising and marketing strategies had nose-dived our expenses into a pool of irrevocable damage. When researching about the startups before I had to meet Mr. Kuber, I had heard that after the seed funding, the next step comes to Series A funding that helps to strengthen operations and build the business after initial establishment. "It makes sense for us to approach for the next level funding too. There is no other way we could stay afloat," Chintan had mentioned for the hundredth time that week. I knew he had a point. But I also did not know how to approach Mr. Kuber with this, considering there had been nothing to show for our business development. However, dreading, I requested an appointment with him. The idea was to show him the next steps – to make sales pitches to people who had enquired, to aggressively focus on business development with the funds acquired, apart from clearing the humongous marketing debts we had accumulated. There was money we still had to pay to Swapna Lok for VR advertising as well. And I don't even want to get into the details of all the printing and publishing costs we had incurred with the intergalactic press. "Our monthly *akashwani* charge has been high due to prime-time airing. We still have to clear the invoices of the last three months; otherwise, they will pull back all content and slap us with a hefty penalty!" Chintan had explained, not unduly paranoid. I was hopeful that he would find it a viable methodology. Once the debts were cleared, we would still have sufficient funds to start elevating our product with direct business development efforts with travel agencies across the galaxies. However, these were a lot of assumptions based on the possibility that we would, in fact, get any more funds. My worst dreads were to come true soon.

Let me tell you upfront, the meeting was a disaster. There's no point sugar coating it. First of all, he didn't give me an in-person appointment. He asked me for a VR interaction, since he was travelling for an audit to Dev Lok; apparently, they had superseded their budget by a big margin because of product renovation. Dev

Lok was trying to reform environmental strength for planet earth that seemed to be losing its immune system. However, this crisis had not been accounted for and had caused major unplanned expenses. Clearly, there was a lot more for me to learn! Anyway, the meeting was short and simple, albeit a grilling one.

"Can you give a quick glance at the business you have done in the last three months?" he asked in an eerily calm tone. I only had to switch the display page on the profit and loss account when he stopped in a voice metallic cold. "Is there anything on that page that you can account as profit?" I did not have an answer. His eyes piercing me with analysis, the next questions shot right through. "Where has the major share of your expense gone?" You know that feeling when you have an answer and you know it is not the right one? That is the moment when you see clearly how wrong you have been.

I whispered a shy word in response, "Marketing." Lastly, he asked me what I was doing for assessment. I couldn't choose between saying 'nothing' or simply staring into space in silence. Three curt questions had it all laid down for me. I knew we had spent brazenly in creating noise, got no work done and had no idea what was going wrong. "Can you justify any expense as worthy of the handsome investment I had made in your glamorous startup?" came the last nail in the coffin. Honestly, after these questions, I had neither the courage nor, thankfully, the stupidity to ask him anything about funding; he would probably have been disappointed me even more then. His parting suggestion had been for me to do a damage assessment, to find out what was going wrong and only then contemplate investing any more money in the business. With a heavy heart, I came back to the darkness of my room. I had managed to disappoint the one man who had shown so much faith in me. And now, it was time to find out how I had made such a holy mess out of it. Chintan and Srijan seemed to echo each other's shock at Mr. Kuber's reaction.

"But it was a well-contemplated move to attract attention. How else were people expected to know about business?" Chintan had questioned.

Srijan had also reasoned with the strong impact that the strategy had managed to create, "Across galaxies, there's nobody who hasn't heard of us! Nobody else has ever managed to create this kind of a buzz!" While their claims were right, I was beginning to realize it wasn't what we needed at that stage. With whatever remained of my energy and funds, I hired a market research company Karma Unlimited, recommended by Narada. The brand was known for their expertise around the universe – baseline study or design of earth, averting the catastrophe of apocalypse when the demons had set to attack the Dev Lok, or the most recent market evaluation for communication strategy to determine the *Kalyug* launch, these all had Karma's footprint on them. The head of creative management and CEO of the Universe, Brahma had been strongly recommended by Lakshmi Aunty, who was patiently helping us out in our hour of crisis. Brahma was known for the light. We were in darkness; it was the most divine calling to seek his advice on what was going wrong with us.

With her referral, we met, explained our predicament and asked for a full-fledged evaluation for what went wrong and what needed to be set right to get the business on track. The evaluation involved interviews with all the stakeholders, existing and potential clients, completion analysis in the market and qualitative analysis with the end users, i.e. the actual tourists who were intended to be the rightful target for the product. The research was an extensive one, spread over personal interviews, group discussions and quantitative surveys through a range of audience across the galaxies. It was expensive as heaven, a lot more than I had anticipated or could even afford, frankly. "But this is true value for money," Brahma had claimed, "It is supposed to set you back on the right track." This apt 'investment', as I was told, was necessary, and hence, the last bits of the seed fund, and some money of my own, were spent into finding out what had gone wrong.

After three months of research, I got a call from the research assistant, asking for a meeting to brief us with the research results. These months had been a stress time for me. We had had to slow down on expenses exorbitantly. This meant that no new expenditures could be made; no product development could be done. We even had to majorly downsize on our interns and work out of my house, desperately trying to acquire a client to make ends meet.

"This meeting will set things right," Srijan had anticipated. "We'll know what to do next and give us a focus." Chintan had, on the other hand, anticipated that this may make matters more complex, if the results came out worse than we expected. Whatever, it was, we went for the meeting. The first thing Brahma said to us, after the initial orientation with the processes followed, was this – "I wish you had come to us earlier, Ganesha. This kind of research is extremely handy before you make the actual spending on the strategies or even before investments into the product building," he said. My heart was already sinking to the bottom of my stomach when he started explaining the various gaps and drawbacks that Shrishti had pulled itself into. Amidst a lot of technical jargons and startup principles thrown into our face, two things clearly stuck out to me. One, simply put, that as a startup, we had made our experiments more valuable than our survival. This meant that our expenditure had superseded in cost to a level that it could cost us our survival. In the name of being big and popular, we had completely sidelined the reality at hand, which we were only running on seed funding, without actual income flow rolled out yet. The second – our homework had been weak, biased and incomplete.

"This is a complete shocker!" Chintan exclaimed. He was the one who had actually gone out there and researched in the market while the product was being developed. "I checked with many travel agencies, tech developers and even tourist departments about the model we were working on. They seemed in awe with the idea," he enunciated. However, some harm had come out of this incomplete work we had begun the venture with. Among other things that were to follow about the reasons for the failure of our startup, these two factors had stuck out voraciously. It was time to evaluate these mistakes and understand what the major wrong turns had been.

Like little children, without the knowledge or experience of what we were diving into or what mattered, I sat down with my faculties of logic and creativity – Chintan and Srijan, equally intrigued – before Brahma to understand all that there was to know.

"Have you heard about the stories of Rahu and Ketu?" he asked in the beginning. I remember them as major influencers of emotional quotient of people. That is to say, they have immense control over the human emotions based on their relative position in the constellations. Anyone in the extra-terrestrial marketing space knows that emotions drive most decisions in the earthly system. A rise in their stock value differently influences human behavior and well-being depending on how much influence, or how many stocks have been purchased. But Brahma had more to tell.

"Many years ago, Rahu and Ketu used to be one single being. The arrogance and evil in this being led to its own downfall when Vishnu chopped the head off," he explained. Apparently, the head and body of this demon had gone ahead and attached themselves to parts of two snakes. One attaching itself in the head's position and the other, the body, thus forming two completely different creatures. "You would think that this made them into two complete beings, but you couldn't be more wrong!" In the process of over achieving, the creature forgot to assess whatever was wrong and ended up creating more damage than good. Brahma explained how Ketu had taken the head of the snake while Rahu became a head on a snake's body. He further compared these two newly conceived creatures as a symbol of the mistakes we had made with Shrishti. Just like Rahu, we had become a mind full of ideas in isolation, not understanding that the ideas need to address the need and demand of the target audience. Blinded by our impression of VR, we had put all our effort into trying to install it into the lives of people without understanding the perspective of the people!

"You say you worked on market research, right?" Brahma asked Chintan, "Did you assess the actual need of the primary users of your product at all?" Chintan's shocked silence was enough to explain to us our biggest mistake! We had developed an entirely new concept and model, assuming that it was the best that potential tourists would get, not considering if this is what they would necessarily want. "You must understand that your ideas, isolated from the environment you want to set them up in, are redundant and unwanted like Rahu's influence on human lives," Brahma's simplification helped me understand how our homework had been incomplete by completely ignoring the most important aspect of understanding what our target audience wanted and whether our so called perfect solution fit into their needs.

"That explains why we have had so many enquiries, but no converting customers!" Srijan had a moment of realization. The travel agencies did not find the product fitting into their business; neither did the tourists find the need of this VR model in their lives! You would think that could be the most basic mistake one could make for their startup. We get so dissolved in passion of our expertise, our likings or simply our hardwork that we forget that we may not be the right piece of puzzle that our audience is looking to fit.

With this realization, Brahma moved to the more strategic flaw of Shrishti's efforts. "I want you to understand that seed funding is critical in establishing the business and rolling it into a state of operations where it can start sustaining itself," he established the beginning of his next point. "Do you see where your expenditure fit anywhere into this equation?"

Chintan was quick to respond, "Our strategy was to create enough buzz and brand value that people would leave aside all competition and come to us for their travel solutions." We were explained then that while marketing and brand value are important aspects in expansion of a startup, these elements are more critical for Series A or B proceedings, when actual operations have become established and there is a deliberate action to aggressively capture the market, beat competition or to remind customers about how effective you are as a brand. "Now tell me, have you reached a stage where you can think about expansion, or beating completion?" My head was hung in disbelief and shame. The answer was obviously no. "Like Ketu, who, without a head, was a body rolling into actions, you kept on investing into your marketing gimmicks without putting your head into what needed to be achieved," Brahma continued.

The essence was that our focus of spending the money should have been in appropriating our product and business development instead of creating noise on a product that had not even entered the market. I admitted I had been too vulnerable with the glamour of the bigger organizations like Vishnu's Cosmo Consultancy or Shukracharya's Online Training platform. I wanted to ape their aggressive marketing techniques and declare to the universe how awesome Shrishti was. "But you see these names you mentioned have worked for centuries to set up their name and faith amidst people. Only now, that they have enough credibility and sustenance in the market do they afford such expenditures," reiterated Brahma, drilling some sense into my Ketu'd understanding of marketing. So we had become so expensive with our glamour quotient that actual and active business seeking had taken a back seat on our investment strategy. That's a common mistake that most new-age startups in the galaxy have been making – not choosing where to invest or planning the strategies with long-term sustenance in mind. The key, as Brahma explained, is in assessing what the priority of expenditure should be and what it's return would be like in the short and long-term plan.

These two major mistakes had torn us apart like the demon that broke into Rahu and Ketu. Instead of assessing what was the essence of our idea or the strategy of our startup, we had isolated our idea from the body of our market and mindlessly worked on a strategy of marketing, thus leading for the very kick start to be an inefficient and superfluous one. What really should have happened was that this assessment and unbiased purview should have been established as an essential homework, before anything began. There was a lot more to learn, many more truths and realizations to hit us in the face. But enough for one day, we parted with Brahma up until the next debriefing session, to find out more.

Moral – *The critical period of kick-starting your startup is meant to establish yourself as an entity that is relevant and can sustain by itself by rolling profitable business. The homework phase should be the most thorough action to make an unbiased understanding of the product as imagined in the audience environment, in the way it is perceived by its end user and in what form may it be of relevance for consumption. Only then can you credit yourself as worthy for existing, let alone seeking growth for strengthening and expansion. It is extremely important to analyze expenditure plans, cleanse priorities with immediate outputs and long term outcomes of those expenditures. Without these insights, there is no promise of sustenance or even survival, as you stand at the brink of being the cause of your downfall.*

6

As You Sow, So Shall You Grow – an approach to startups

*T*here was once a huge ceremony in Brahmaputra on Mount Meru, where Brahma lives. Many deities, Gods and choicest devotees had been invited. It was one of the largest *yagya* being conducted for the betterment of the universe. My parents had taken me to the ceremony on the condition that I wouldn't throw things into the holy fire. "It has much deeper implications," my mother had said. That was the first time ever that I had the privilege of watching Aunt Saraswati, glowing with knowledge, peace and tranquility, sitting poised by the fire, chanting mantras along with Brahma as all and sundry sat around the pier and offered everything ranging from flowers and leaves to wood and grains to the growing fire. '*Ahuti*' or offerings, as they called it, were immersed into the blaze as symbols of irrevocable surrender.

"Careful of what you think and offer to the holy fire because whatever goes '*swaha*' in it, you must not ask back!" One of the old sages had pointed out to us children.

Back then, I had no idea about the deeper meanings of our prayers and practices, but as I watched the proceedings of the yagya, I wondered to myself why anyone would simply throw things into the fire, why it was impossible to bring those things back and whether the glare of the pier spread into our lives in ways we could not see or understand. All I understood was the glamour and poise of the moment, the collection of important people and curiosity that all of it invoked in me, even as a child, to know how we would all end up if our wishes surrendered in the yagna came true. "You will grow into a dynamic and successful power, by the grace of the holy fire," Aunty Sarawasti had blessed me benignly.

But after all these years, as I sat analyzing everything happening around me, I understood that every day, every step and every effort made for Shrishti had been a yagya or *yajna* as people popularly call it; a yagya that was asking offerings from me. Whether these things came in the form of my time, our funding, ideas or resources spent recklessly in the heat of the moment, the fire, like a giant black hole, took everything in.

I was just wondering if unlike others sitting through those offerings on Mount Meru all those years ago, I had been blinded and ignorant to the might of the power and contrary to my mother's continued warnings, had I simply offered irrevocable, irreplaceable assets in the name of business investments. After spending a grilling day at Lord Brahma's office, I had come to realize that Shrishti had been built on several flaws and illusions. But all this while, I had felt that the investments were made with correct insight and intensions, if nothing else. As it turns out, I was wrong all along. Hesitantly, I summoned my confidants,

Srijan and Chintan and we headed to the office once again, to embrace the rest of the briefing that Karma – the company we had hired for our assessment – had diagnosed for us. To say that the session of the day before had been painful would be an understatement. Not only had our market strategies and operation policies been dismissed and criticized for being reckless, our brain child, the business model of VR, had also been brutally scorned for the lack of insight and market evaluation. We had learned that our investments had been out of line with priority, that our management team had been unorganized that our market research was negligent and disrespectful of the target audience; big blows for a small startup. As we walked into the office, we realized, there were more to come.

"Do you know what Sunk Cost is?" Brahma asked at the onset. I was new to the world of entrepreneurship and was still unaware of many technical terms and theories of the business world. Whatever it was, from where I stood, sunk cost did not sound like a positive term. He further explained that this was the cost that could not be recovered once invested. In many situations, it was not necessarily a bad thing, if well placed; investments could convert into long term assets. Clearly, that wasn't the case with us. Our sunk costs had been plenty and mostly with no lucrative effect. The product development expenditures, the research budget and most critically, the marketing whale that we had hoped to sail on had all amounted to unaffordable sunk costs. Is this what the yagya had been like? I wondered as *Brahmadoots* displayed presentations on investment plans that could have brought us better return of investment. These were the offerings we had made into the pier of our startup without even calculating quantitatively how each aspect would emerge as a result. As it turns out, instead of showing profit, our foolhardiness had resulted in counterproductive consequences.

As Brahma continued that day's session, he brought us to the next point on the research result. "A critical understanding that comes with experience is to know your market, to know how the leaders in your market function and what you offer as competition." When Brahma had set out to form humans on Earth, he had analyzed the available resources, the existing form of lives, celestial or demonic, and he had evaluated the competition that came in form of other life creators across the galaxies. We understood from their success and failures and identified the relevant edge that would keep humans on top of the chain as the head of life-forms.

"But our VR technology is unique and edgy!" Chintan retaliated, "We have a state of the art program put into place and I am not saying this out of arrogance, we really are good at this!" I felt that urgent sense of protest as well. But after the previous day's eye-opening session, some of my arrogance had been broken down and I was ready to listen.

"The reason why you stand nowhere close to your competition is not because your product is inferior in quality," Brahma explained, "It is because you have been building it without the insight of what works for your competitors." To understand the relevance of a product, Brahma explained, it turns out, that you need to introduce your beta product, in its rough cut version. This helps to understand whether the environment is ready to accept it or not. Srijan, I could tell, was squirming at the idea of releasing something without perfection. I was curious too.

"Do you know what I did when I first started working on the project human? I made Manu 1.0," he explained that instead of simply setting up a large scale manufacturing unit for humans, he released a prototype into the earth's environment to see how it worked. "The focus was not to launch the most perfect man but to see what it takes to make a perfect man, relevant for the earth's environment." Now that made sense. We hadn't done that at all! So submerged in perfecting our product to the bits, we never thought about testing it outside of our lab environment.

"Wait a minute! Is that why Shatrupa was born sometime later and only then the human population began its growth?" Chintan had hit it spot on. Shatrupa was Brahma's alpha launch, Human 2.0 with all the corrections and customization that needed to complete the shortcomings of Manu 1.0.

"It is not the imperfection you should be afraid of, sons, but the resistance to accept that your product maybe flawed and will need to be beaten up, melted and reshaped many times over." In that one sentence, he had given us the simple process of forming gold.

I could tell that Chintan was still struggling with this idea of an imperfect product. I encouraged him to ask. This is one more thing I had learned over time now, that making mistakes and asking questions would only help to clean the track for the final race. Better be rugged and bumpy before the race than crash and tumble at the end of it! "O creator of creatures, I am stuck with wonder and yet, something puzzles me. With all your expertise, you got human 2.0, right, and that was sufficient to keep your successful models going. But what do we do until we get the right product, how do we sustain?" You know that omnipotent smile that only gods or mothers can flash? Brahma was wearing one of those. "I am glad you ask this, Chintan, because the next point of Karma's research is just that." I have to admit, that by now, these revelations had stopped feeling like blows and begun to sink in like life lessons. I could feel my mind broadening, my ears enlarging, as though I was more open to listening, I could feel my senses heightening, as though I was ready to smell and absorb everything I could learn. I didn't dread hearing the upcoming learnings anymore.

I listened on, making notes in my head, "Your business model needs to be designed in a way that it can sustain your experimental process. Hit and miss will continue, and frankly it is important to be continuously evolving to make a better product." Brahma explained that when he had launched Manu, he observed whether or not he would have relevance in earth's environment, what his USP would be, what was attractive about him for other creatures to accept him as their leader. With these practical answers, without much gung-ho in terms of the luster of a brand or marketing, he went on to work on the alpha version. No extra expenditure, no diversion of focus. "If your audience is beginning to understand and accept your product, even its rough cut, beta version, you can probably assume that in its finished form, your product will be able to pick up well." Oops! I thought in my strangely enlarging head as he laid it down, that I had been doing just the opposite.

"I was so busy focusing on what to tell people that I forgot to focus on my business."

It is ironical that I said it at that moment because I could see the Brahmadoot smiling as he switched to the next planetary configuration on the sky. I liked Brahma's presentation skills a lot. He always made things simple, practical and attractive when talking to his clients. For our presentation, he had set up a virtual planet hopping theme where each of the learning presented itself in front of us as though happening live on a planet. "So much for calling myself a virtual reality expert," thought I. When the next subject came on, I felt the irony. 'What is your focus?' said the star formation. "On the contrary, dear Ganesha," Brahma spoke gently. Was his tone getting milder or was I becoming less resistant to listening?

"The mantra to a successful business is to focus all your attention listening to people and letting that build your business model, he continued explaining." His explanation went on with the example of planet earth where you will find that most successful entrepreneurs, from the old age teachers running *gurukuls*, to the newest tech-gurus, focused on their customers, paid keen attention to their grievances and feedback and addressed those before beating their own drum. The reason for many startups to fail is because they get too aggressive about securing funding or being on top of the marketing chart, instead of putting the customer first. "Why do you think there are so many dead and deserted planets in Milky Way alone?" Because people were trying too hard to do business, looking at each other's planet, and forgot about what its habitants would need and want. If you have been able to tap into the need of your customer and show them that you're listening and you care more for them than the commercial hunger of your business, you will find more loyal, understanding and even forgiving customers.

You see, friends, how grossly wrong we had been in the basics of our business ideal? We barely listened. No wonder my ears had been growing strangely in the last few hours, as though my whole was body was responding to the teachings of Brahma.

It is weird though that while I could feel myself growing calmer and more comfortable with the elaboration of my own failure, Chintan and Srijan seemed to be getting more and more restless with every whack of the word. "But we did all that marketing to bring people to us. We needed to be loud and clear that we are here to help you with our services. What more could we have done?" Srijan was pleading almost desperately. And yet that smile never faded.

"You are right, little one. You did bring many people to you. Your data also reveals that the number of enquiries that came in with your marketing launch was unlike any other seen in the galaxy for a startup launch that hasn't even tested its product." Brahma enlightened us. "If you're at the registration desk of your new apartment at heaven, would you just want many people to keep ringing bells and leave or would you like more people to come and register as potential clients, if not immediate ones?" You would obviously want them to stick around, I answered in my head. What we needed was stickiness, not a cluster of uninformed or untargeted enquiry. Brahma explained that our priority should have been to perhaps build a single case model, implement it with some prominent travel agents and attract more business to try it out. Not just create a huge buzz around Shrishti with nothing to retain the watching audience.

"That was our sunk cost," I spoke finally, "It wasn't going anywhere until we had used it to build a retentive customer base or stickiness." All the Brahmadoots and the lord himself stood nodding in approval. Chintan and Srijan, standing with their backs at these learned array of celestials, could not see what I saw, the realization of all the foolhardiness that had blinded us into the glamour of creating a name but not really knowing how to power that name with our product.

The day's session had come to an end. But as darkness approached from the horizon, I felt a light rising inside of me. My head felt heavy, but not with burden. I realized that with this failure, I was coming to understand a lot more about my business than I had learned during the actual course of operating it. My intellect was widening, my reception of feedback was expanding with a readiness to listen and absorb. It felt like I was changing into someone else – a new person with a new perspective.

The equation was getting simpler and clearer now. To pick up from where we had left the day before, where shock and dismay had been drowning me, I could find good sense prevailing. What a sharp contrast! Only because, as Brahma has said, I was not afraid of being proven wrong anymore, because I could now correct myself and become better. Isn't that the whole point of any mission we undertake? Whether it is friendships, relations, education, jobs or your enterprise. The idea is to work on a goal and yet know that many times the path you will choose will be the wrong one. The fact that you will make mistakes should not deter you from making them, but make you more aware and ready to learn from them. If you focus in the service instead of the gain, the benefit will come running to you at the end anyway. This is what I learned from Karma.

It is the large and wise mountains that sit silently and build their strength without the pomp. Little streams keep gushing and gurgling, making a lot of noise and drawing attention towards them, but with little strength. Everyone goes to watch and admire the ocean, because it has depth and value for everyone, because like the mountains too, it silently listens and provides. I could see it clearly now; it was all around me; in nature, in the cosmos, in gods and their creations, in learnings and failures. I didn't have to shine or try to attract people, not yet at least. I had to listen to them, I had to focus on what they wanted and fit it with what I had to offer. A successful business, like earth, above all other planets, or humans, above all other life forms, succeeded because it was allowed to be examined in the environment. Respectfully, when you watch the audience accept, reject or analyze your product, you prove that you are ready to listen, to accept the flaws and to rightfully evolve into a better business.

Moral – It doesn't matter what your product is about and how well you have constructed it unless you have learned from it in its desired environment. That is why it is wise to test your idea in the real world instead of building castles in the air of isolation. The target audience is the business building block; you ignore that and nothing about your model will stand. The dedication, in the beginning of your startup, should be in building a loyal and appreciative customer-base that can be earned with your loyalty in return. Once stickiness is built, the business will automatically follow. Instead of forcing your ideas down on your audience, keep your ears and eyes open and try to read what the market is sharing and only based on that should you make your decisions about the product design, business model and marketing strategies.

7

We, the People – a resource worth many lessons

*T*hey say who you are is defined by who you are with. Shrishti was basically a composition of my inner consciousness, a mix of my strengths and weaknesses, and therefore, it was all me.

I remember growing up, my mother used to tell me stories about the creation of the universe. Especially when there were times I was disappointed with the cruelty of people or got upset when my friends did not want to listen to my opinion, Ma would sit me down and tell me this particular story about what makes up the world and all the people in it.

"Do you know how all these different kinds of creatures came to life, Ganesha?" she would ask handing me one of my favourite *laddoos* to calm me down. Having heard the stories a few times over, I knew the answer. But I would always let her tell it in her own, magical way. "From various parts of the mighty Lord Vishnu's body, came out the several forms of life. As different types of humans were formed, the almighty gave each of them specific characteristics and specialty based on the need of human kind."

"What kinds of humans did he make, Ma?" I would ask. "They would be warriors and craftsmen, leaders and helpers, teachers and businessmen… all kinds of humans, son." She would explain with kindness that all the diversity that exists in this world was for the benefit of the universe. "Can you imagine how boring, lifeless and one-dimensional life would be if every single celestial being was built alike?" I would nod appreciatively. This story always helped me remind myself of the bigger perspective of life. I understood that you need different kinds of people, skills and perspectives to bring a wholesome approach to life.

Growing up, my father Shiva would make a point to introduce me to various gods and deities across galaxies. Do you know how many are there? There's one for power, one of knowledge, one for water, one for fire, one for rage and one for mercy too! "Because we are smart gods, son. We believe in specialization and delegation.

For eons, the whole higher management of the cosmos has progressed effectively based on this mantra. If you pay attention to the details, you have the best business management strategies waiting to be learned from. And this is exactly what the next lesson in Lord Brahma's conference hall was about. When Chintan, Srijan and I walked into the Karma conference hall number 1000 that day, we were surprised to see the head chair empty. But as soon as the attendance was complete, the sky blinked to signal and there, with all his might, Brahma appeared on the panel from another galaxy. "I am sorry for not being there in flesh and blood, but I have another investment to assess in this part of the universe and I do not like to miss opportunities of universe travel. On a more serious note, there were some quality assurance investigations to be made. I hope it is ok that I am handling our meeting from a distance." He winked through his best charming smile. Lesson number one, right there – actively taking part in whatever is necessary, no matter how far you have to go or what level of involvement you have to prove. That is what leads to the beginning of the review that Brahma had for us for that day. "The theme of today is Human Resources," he declared. The most important element of an organization is the people that bring the organization together. "I want you to pay close attention to what has been the strength and weaknesses of the human resources of Shrishti," he directed. And then, he led me through a series of questions about the various issues Shrishti had not paid attention to in the realm of the right resources for the right tasks. "There is a reason for every star in the constellation, a purpose for every branch on a tree." He went on to explain how each person in an employee plays a specific role and serves an intended purpose in the machinery of an organization. This essence had been taken severely for granted by us at Shrishti. We had people working for us, mostly interns. I remember conversation with the team being more about what needed to be done at hand instead of what is efficiently possible and by whom. For any task needed to be done, Chintan's rhythmic statement was, "I'll get an intern to do it." That every employee, intern or fulltime, be oriented and given a purpose is the first and foremost priority for any organization. "One of the most important aspects to keep in mind before hiring someone is what purpose you see them serving in the organization; their bigger goal and their smaller tasks need to designed and defined in order for this purpose to be met."

On the other hand, what we had were a bunch of people running errands for us as and when they came up. It had never occurred to me that I needed to pay attention to the people in the organization for them to be able to pay attention to the organization. Almost echoing my thoughts, Brahma spoke again, "You know how your father's strength lies in his eye, that though shut, sees and understands everything?" I nodded. "Similarly, in business management, the perspective of the 'I' is extremely important. There are three actions that need to be taken when it comes to business management." I listened on curiously at the new array of information being delivered, making mental notes and comparisons to our treatment of human resources in Shrishti.

The Creator went on to explain that the most important aspect of human resources, the first 'I' was initiation. The first thing to do would be to align the motivation and mission of your employees with that of the organization. It is imperative that each element of the organization understand the vision and find themselves agreeing to it. "If that does not happen, you will tend to lose focus or find people straying," his voice came as a warning, "More importantly, you do not make the best of your resources when they are floating aimlessly instead of being dedicated to goals. This first step of initiation is what brings your employees upbeat with the mutual expectations. It is an important step that needs to be taken even at the time of recruitment, to understand the anticipations and the orientation of a resource. "Every hire you make is an investment. It deserves due diligence and respect." As Brahma's voice echoed in from the sky, I looked around at each of the Brahmdoots who appeared at ease, comfortable and inclined towards each moment being spent in that hall. I saw understanding of what was going on and I saw an eagerness to learn more.

"Right hires," I whispered to Srijan reading his expressions echoing my own. My instinct was to compare how much time I had spent on even considering if I was working with the right set of people. Here was another example, sitting right in front of my eyes, proving to me how simple, basic considerations play such a critical role in the flow of your business.

As the concept of 'Initiation' began sinking in, Brahma moved to the next level of perspective. As usual, his lessons came with fabulous examples of the universe, both simplifying and legitimizing the points he made. "Ravana, the king of Lanka had many reasons that led to his downfall. But as a king, the downfall of his rule came because he was not a good ruler." Many times, the advisors came to Ravana to tell him about the war situation, to give him warning about the unrest in the court, but he paid no heed. As a bad manager, he was not involved with his employees with open ears and an open mind. As Brahma talked more about Ravana, my mind drifted to his contemporary, Lord Ram, known till date as one of the best managers and leaders in the history of Indian kings. I was lost in these thoughts when Brahma suddenly turned his head to me and asked, "Ganesha, can you give me an example of a good manager, on the other hand?"

"Lord Ram!" came my prompt reply.

"And why do you think he was a good one?"

By now, I had understood the point in consideration. I thought through and answered with poise. "He was a democratic leader, he listened to his people and he got himself involved in everyday lives of both his courtesans as well as his subjects.

A nodding approval met with, "Exactly... he was connected both with his end users as well as his employees. He acted as an interim part of his team instead of merely heading them like a boss." To understand the opinion and concerns of your employees, to engage with them at a level of empathy and synchronicity and to be able to comprehend their point of view before making critical decisions. Lord Ram was a people's man. His presence was found amidst his people, being an interim part of their governance, their decisions and hurdles, all with his first-hand participation. "And do you know what is lacking now, in your approach and methodology?" He asked softly from galaxies away.

"This must be how he manages such a large scale of events," I later found myself marveling to Srijan and Chintan. He makes sure that his presence is ensured in every element where he is required, irrespective of what his other engagements are. Do you know why they call him the '*Chidakash*'? Perhaps because he is as omnipresent as the sky and always conscious and mindful of not only his own thoughts and actions, but also of those who comprise his team. 'As present and wise as the sky'- a quality that will only do good for you if you decide to initiate any run anything, a family, the universe or simply, an enterprise.

Apart from being extremely meticulous in his planning and strategy, he also ensures that he actively participated in everything that his team engages in. A lesson, valuable in its implementation and in fact one that needs to be become an imperative part of any entrepreneur's system. "It is one thing to assign tasks to your team and simply assess the results and altogether another thing to walk with them through the process and keep yourself involved with the perspectives, challenges and achievements of your team."

"So does that mean we should be managing the team members at a step-by-step level, administering control through every level?" Chintan asked perturbed. I could feel myself echoing this sentiment. Wouldn't that mean micro-managing everything? And doesn't that make me a bad leader?

"I understand your confusion and I am glad you are thinking in this direction." I could sense a benign lesson to follow.

"Do you feel that you have to make most of the decisions for your employees?" he asked.

"Yes, I do. In fact, it turns out to be extremely time-consuming." I replied in earnest.

"Do you feel that you have seen very little growth in your employees in terms of their capacity and skill for taking initiatives?"

"Oh, for certain! It feels like every direction has to be instructed, every input provided to them, though once that is done, they are willing to work hard to produce an output," Chintan replied with most experience in dealing with our team which honestly had mostly interns and then some consultants who came on-board on need basis.

"You see what I am saying?"asked Brahma, "You do not have to micro-manage your team, you just have to be in sync with them. Staying involved does not mean you do their work for them. On the very contrary, it means that you encourage them, with insight and deliberation, to make their own decisions and to build their own skills." He went on to explain the process of capacity building of the team by two means. As usual, Brahma's lessons came with examples of the cosmos, about elements that had existed before my eyes for centuries and yet, I had perhaps taken many a details for granted!

His story began with the narration of when many thousands of years ago Mother Earth was in a dilemma because everything seemed to be falling apart, because of the all the evils spreading on earth, people were planning to abandon the planet. The evil elements from the sky would come and attack the good people of the world and escape the planet. "Mother Earth watched with helplessness as the mortals struggled to catch these evils, or themselves trying to escape earth to end the ordeal," Brahma narrated. At this stage, Mother Earth came to the *Trimurti* (the combined powers of Lord Brahma, Lord Vishnu and Lord Shiva) to help her out of this ordeal. There had to be a way out to put an end to this struggle. "What do you think the Trimurti did? Do you think they went and fought the battles of earth for her? Do you think they got the humans to come to them for every complain, begging for resolutions?" I had a feeling I had heard of this story from my childhood, owing to Ma's amiable and animated story-telling skills.

"Is this the story of the birth of Gravity?" I asked inquisitively? I could tell from the pleased smile on Brahma's face that I was right. "It was gravity that brought everybody back to Mother Earth. She managed to keep everybody's focus on the core, to have them come to her for consultation; she engaged everybody, but without making it too obvious to them. Gravity worked in the background, encouraging people to take their own leaps, but held them strong, lest they may lose control. On the other hand, she kept a close control on the evils that flew into her atmosphere, allowing nothing to escape from her attention." That made perfect sense. The idea of involvement then meant that you stay connected, while giving space and encouragement to your employees to make their own decisions and engage them into taking initiatives.

"So then, the key is to listen?" I thought more to myself rather than asking Brahma. I didn't need his nod that followed generously to tell me that I had figured it out. It was in fact when I had listened to my interns that I had got to know about the fact that we were not converting any enquiries into business, which revealed the actual plethora of issues that Shrishti had fallen into.

Lastly, Brahma told me to focus on who was managing what in the enterprise. There will be different people with different expertise and a good leader will be able to maneuver these varied capacities into the appropriate position and scope. Both as a leader as well as a team member, it was the duty of a founder to match the need with the provision. I reflected back on what had been the situation in the organization. Nandi uncle had been the one managing the abundant and hardworking team of interns. Although, I have to admit, I had felt the gap between what we expected from such a large team of interns and what we received as an outcome owing to the amount of time we had to spend spoon-feeding every little instruction. That was simply because Nandi Uncle had no knowledge about VR. How could I expect him to make decisions on the subject then? It was a simple folly, committed at my end that had completely disconnected me from the team and their inputs.

Further to the point, Brahma looked intently at me and then added, "And once you have positioned the right people at the right place, your real work begins..." and all this while I had been thinking that we were done with discussing the most critical step (and in Shrishti's case, a very critical flaw) for a successful enterprise. I clearly had a lot more to learn! Coming to the point, Brahma began with asking what Shrishti had done so far to enhance capacity and to improve the systems for efficient functioning of the employees. "What do you do to ensure a conducive and effective environment for your team?" I didn't have too much as a response. But I do know that the daily exercise we engaged in with the entire team would count for something at least. And it did. "Yes, that is a very effective method to keep in touch with your employees. But it amounted to nothing more than a regulated reporting system, albeit a useful one." It was a very certain fact that our morning ritual to engage with the entire team was an efficient way to understand the current status of the assignments that had been appointed to them. However, what it did to increase their capacity and effectiveness, I couldn't say for sure. I waited eagerly for his readings that would lead to a solution for this issue.

"If an organization does not set its targets with the team and does not, subsequently inculcate an aspirational environment to work towards the said target, one is bound to get complacent and lose track of progress." What he continued to elaborate was that there is a need for any team to indulge into a healthy competitive and inquisitive streak to ensure continuous and regular growth. One needs regular targets, assessment of those targets, comparison with other performers and consequent evaluation of the strengths and weaknesses, opportunities and challenges cumulatively as a team. A regular process of mentoring, monitoring and evaluation has manifold purposes to serve in a startup. "Not only do you understand the efficiency of your employees and are able to assess and calculate the kinds of challenges the team would face, this is also a very effective mechanism to ensure that learning from one case can be shared with the entire team," Brahma said wisely, "Most importantly, you are connected with the actual developments on each front. This way, no issue or challenge comes as a surprise for you and you can be better prepared." I could not help but nod. Had I simply kept myself in the loop with my team, encouraged them to share their challenges and to match each other and compete with their respective targets, two things would have clearly happened. Firstly, that there are no conversions from enquiries to contracts would have come out clearly. Secondly, had conversion targets been set, and incentivized competitions designed, we would have had a much more efficient process of covering the business generation aspect of the startup.

"Your people are your backbone, Ganesha," Bhrama began with the conclusion. "If you think you can simply work on your own, you are wrong. If you think you can simply hire people and expect them to take it from there, you are wrong. And if you think you can simply alienate yourself from your employees and let your own tasks take all your time, you are most definitely wrong." Each statement came down on me like a much needed blow. Just like my mother used to lovingly pull my ears when giving me the most important lessons, I felt learning from Brahma coming with a gentle pull on my ears, elongating my earlobes and expanding my receptivity. I had many more things to learn, but for that one session, I had picked up some important details that I had missed out on in formation of Shrishti. As I walked home that night, beside Chintan and Srijan, I glimpsed at all the simple yet fatal flaws in us (and therefore in me, since the two were my own creativity). I could see now that the line between you and your employee, especially in a startup, is really thin and cannot be ignored in its points of separations and blends. The rule of the universe also applies equally to the rule of a startup – 'there is no other'. That you must exercise all practices with your employees as you will with yourself; that you must not view them as someone else, but as extensions of yourself. With these lessons, I found myself finding a new definition of the expression 'a people's person' because that is what it would take to succeed in a space where people are your backbone.

Moral – *Employees demand a very serious consideration for a startup, where systems are still being set-up, culture still being built and lessons still being learnt. Generating an equation with your employees where transactions of opinions and issues can take place smoothly is of extreme significance. It must be ensured that while space and environment for initiatives and decision making is allowed for individual capacity building, as a leader, it is imperative that your participation and support forms encouragement, and at the same time, keeps you in the circuit of all processes in your enterprise. Over all, choose your people wisely, and once they are chosen, employ your strengths and attention at them wisely.*

8

The *Moolah* Magic – a lesson in every success and failure with money

They say that money runs the world. It plays a very important role in all sorts of equations of mortals, and the immortals too! The business of money can make or break relations, build empires or burn down establishments. Our history is full of stories depicting both successes and failures governed by the works of moolah. However, as a celestial growing up amongst all sorts of gods, I had often witnessed several gods visiting the Kailash Parbat, sometimes for work, sometimes for rituals. A very vivid memory that I have from childhood is of the occasion of a certain Deepawali (the Hindu festivals of lights) when everybody had gotten together to participate in the ostentatious Lakshmi-Kuber yagna as a means to worship all forms of wealth and prosperity. I too had gone dressed to become a part of this ritual and observe divinity in all its grandeur. However, when the rituals began, I found that Devi Saraswati and my mother were also seated in places of worship. "I thought we were worshipping and celebrating wealth and prosperity, Baba," I asked my father with a child-like confusion.

"Yes we are, son," came his reply. I could tell that he knew what I was getting at, and yet, the Bhole Nath, in his playful mannerism, still continued to act innocent of my perplexity.

"Then why are the other Devis being worshipped too, Baba?"

At this, he turned attentively at me, ready for one of the conversations, I could tell, where he asks of me to take the lead and reach my own inference before giving his own opinion. "What is Mother Parvati known as a goddess of?" he asked.

"Ma is the goddess of power!" I replied proudly.

"And what is Devi Saraswati the goddess of?" came the next question.

"Devi is the goddess of knowledge," I replied affectionately; she was my personal favourite.

"Do you see what that means? Why they too must be worshipped along with Devi Lakshmi?" My father prodded. I thought for a few moments. Could it mean that the three devis always visited any place together and therefore always needed to be summoned together? I had often noticed that whenever Ma and Devi Saraswati left for their tours around the universe, Devi Lakshmi generally followed suit. I reflected the same thoughts to Baba, enquiring about the relevance of this observation.

"You are absolutely right, dear Ganesha. Wherever Devi Parvati and Devi Saraswati enter, Devi Lakshmi is bound to follow… now the rituals are about to begin, let us take our positions…"

Flashback of that incident came to me the day I was walking towards Karma Enterprise for the next session of debriefing of

Shrishti's analysis. I had been told at the end of the previous session that the subject of economics and financial management was to be discussed next. With the anticipation and evaluation of my own understanding and practice, I dwelled deep into thoughts about it. Wealth and prosperity comes only to those who exercise power and knowledge first. This power could be the power of confidence, the power of will or determination or simply the power of one's opportunity or position that works to one's advantage. Knowledge too comes at several levels – the knowledge of one's capacity, knowledge of one's subject, of the audience of that subject, and very importantly, the knowledge of awareness of challenges and boundaries, of hurdles and environment.

"It is a common misconception that financial mishaps happen only because money was not managed well," Lord Brahma began with the introduction of the subject. In that last few sessions of our debriefing, I had seen a myriad approach to communication from team Karma. The content had always been direct and categorized, the conversation always simple and insightful and the direction always engaging in styles that was relevant to the target audience, a.k.a. team Shrishti. With the help of moderated discussions by Brahma himself, we had derived upon solutions or approaches that could have addressed our issues. Starting from individual and leading up to organizational aspects, we had undertaken a mind-opening journey through understanding universal principals, historical examples and logical conclusions. In all of this, I had been able to conclude at the end of each session, that most of the flaws that led to the failure of Shrishti had been elementary in principle and critical in their purpose. While I had begun to understand that running a startup was a huge responsibility and had its immense load of challenges, I was also gradually learning that most of these challenges could be addressed at a fundamental level simply by keeping in mind and preparing oneself better around the said elements. Out of all the issues, I had imagined financial management to be the most complicated and challenging one. However, as we progressed further into the day, I realized that like every other universal principle, economics too ran on simple fundamental approaches and as long as it was dealt with wisdom and organized determination, financial management could become a good friend and support to you.

"Let us begin from the beginning," Brahma interrupted my chain of thoughts. "What was your first reaction when you received your seed funding from Kuber?"

"That now, a huge burden had been lifted off my shoulder and now I would be able to do anything I wanted and dreamed for Shrishti," I replied candidly.

"Now take a couple of steps back and imagine that instead of Kuber, you yourself had bootstrapped this investment into Shrishti. You had rinsed through every source, resource you could manage and collected this amount to initiate Shrishti's operations." I did so, but not without a shudder in my conscience. I could feel my mind building knots of stress to imagine spending that much money from my own pocket and to bring it to the state that it stood at today. As I felt my mind tense up, I heard his next question echoing my own botheration. "Now, I want you all to ask yourself a question, with reference to each of your department. Think deep and think through… if this was your own money, would you have spent it the way you did with Kuber's money?" I knew the answer in that very instance. Moving backwards in the process, I realized that from the beginning, I had never treated this money with the respect and judiciousness it deserved. At no point during the planning of the expenditure had I ever considered any kind of precautions or paid heed to looking for more economical options at all levels. It was a definite cushion of financial comfort that had come to us with the seed funding. Had this been money squeezed out of our own pockets, I have no doubt that each decision of every spending would have come with its deserved share of laconic insight.

"The same principle should hold true for all capital then. Irrespective of the source of the capital, there has to be accountability of the money being used. The abundance should be used as a tool for futuristic aspiration, not a short-termed curse," I was told.

However, judicious planning was not the only thing to watch out for in the business of moolah. "To be judicious does not mean that you cut down expenses where necessary," warned Lord Brahma with an intensity that commanded attention. Therefore, the crux of financial management was to maintain a balance between control and confidence, both amalgamated in planning. "How did you plan to spend so much money in advertising and marketing?" he asked with genuine interest.

"We needed to create a buzz about the brand in a way that nobody would miss Shrishti. We thought that once a recognition for the brand had been created, we would be able to get many people on board to try out our product, if not start using it immediately," Chintan took over to respond.

"Was this decision discussed, deliberated upon and compared with other points of priority where investments could have been made?"

It wasn't. "This was the first thing that came to our head and felt like the most intelligent and effective way of starting with the investment." Even as Chintan spoke those words, I knew the point that Lord Brahma was trying to make. It wasn't necessary that the first idea would be the best idea; the first option would be the best option, which is what makes deliberation, research and comparison a critical part before an expenditure plan.

"Have you observed that despite there being several planets in our beloved Milky Way galaxy, there's only one planet that has been able to sustain life?" Brahma enquired, indicating that another of his analogies were to be expected in this part of the explanation. "During the process of creation, all the different planets and asteroids were studied and examined for their texture, model, features, benefits and challenges. We didn't go around building earth with the very first whim that came to our head, you know," he added in a critical tone. This is what must be done with business too, I had begun to infer, studying the financial models of competitors, analyzing different approaches and assessing some examples of both successes and failures of startups that range in your sector can be extremely effective in giving you in-depth ideas before diving in with your actual expenditure. "When all the features of all the planets had been examined, to see what worked and what didn't, we had a clear idea through the process of elimination about how and where we would need to 'invest' our skills in order to make a planet ideal for life and sustainability," he continued. We had done no such thing.

"I know you pitched yourself as an altogether different product. But you must not forget that your target audience was still the same, and you were to function in the same environment." That made perfect sense too. It is a huge folly to discount yourself away from your environment, no matter what product or sector you are exploring. Only once you have understood the buying and rejecting habits of your audience, assessed the various designs and their consequences devised by your competitors can you attain complete knowledge to give you the confidence of an investment.

It was an obvious question that came to my head, but I wasn't sure whether it was even sensible enough to ask it. For some reason, Lord Brahma knew my dilemma before I could even frame my own thoughts too well. "You know, Ganesha," he said to me gently, "There are no strictly defined rules between right and wrong in your approach in an enterprise. It is possible that you may be able to devise something that works fine for you but can fail for someone else. Which is why, one mustn't be afraid to take the first steps in innovation and an experiment… what I am saying is, do not be afraid of making mistakes."

This encouraged me to word my concerns. "But lord, look where our mistake have landed us! How are we to know whether the experiments we have made will work or not?"

He smiled at me generously, like a kind teacher patiently picking out each mistake in his student's assignment and helping him correct those. "It is fine to make mistakes, so you can avoid making blunders. When you are testing the temperature of water, do you dive in full length or do you tip your toe at the edge to assess the body reaction?"

We had obviously dived head first with our expenditure. "So you are saying that had we toned down our advertising and marketing strategies and only launched a basic idea to assess the audience reaction, our brand recognition would have managed to bring us business?" Chintan asked critically. I liked the fact that Chintan never settled with any statement or logic until he had examined it from all angles; except, that we had not succeeded in doing this when we were planning our finances.

"No, that is not what would have happened," Brahma replied ever so patiently. "But you would have been able to identify the audience reaction around your product based on your advertisements and been able to gauge that people were not ready for your product. Or rather, that your product, in its existing form, was not ready for the people." And then we wouldn't have gone all out with our expenditures.

Having put this question to rest at our content, Brahma looked at me and asked nudging, "So, Ganesha, are you ready with your question yet?"

I was. "How do you know that the decisions you have made are right or wrong? What is the parameter of assessing the rightness of these investments?" I felt like I was going to sound naïve, not knowing what good or bad decisions are and yet aspiring to run a business. But his reply really calmed my nerves down.

"I am glad you ask, son. Although, like everything else in business, there is no hard and fast rule about what can or cannot work, but while making an investment, two basic mantras can help you determine whether you are on the right course. First of all, it is advisable to determine your course of action based on priorities. Using this as a check-list, you must ensure that you spend your money in that order of purpose; any sign of straying from this course is an indicative of something going wrong (of course, there are unforeseen circumstances or unexpected developments that can require a change of course, but that needs to be accounted for). Secondly, it is a good idea to see what your return of investment would be and whether any investment is bringing its return in the next six months. Especially when you are yet to raise your Series A funding and aggressively expand your operations, judicious utilization of resources should be exercised keeping in mind what each of these will convert into as a return. This is a good way of building a culture of sustenance and bears fruits in the long run."

As I went about the logical step-by-step processes of lessons that Lord Brahma had prepared to educate us in financial management, I watched with wonder how all the presentations went past us with such smooth efficiency that it almost felt like a natural process. The Brahmadoots were all involved in various steps, bringing the right set of documents, setting up the right equipment and connecting one presentation with another seamlessly. I wondered how such efficiency was to be achieved but it didn't take long for me to observe the unsaid guidance that came to each employee involved in the presentation. Having a mentor makes a huge difference in your approach towards an issue. I raised this point out loud for all participants to hear. Lord Brahma picked on this point to further his explanation on financial management. "The *gurukul* culture in our system was setup for this very reason. It wasn't that the children could not read the literature on their own or could not find their way into surviving as adults in this world. But with a guru, one's path is paved in a manner that brings to you the appropriate paths and yet gives you the power of judgment to choose which path you take." Similarly, taking advice from people who hold experiences that you may lack, especially in verticals that are unknown to you, is an approach that comes with great opportunities. Often, people in startups are experts of their subject matter and have relevant experience in designing their products, or even handling operations sometimes. However, more often than not, financial management is not their forte and this leads to a huge gap between business expectations and ultimate reality. I had often felt the dilemma of not knowing the correct approach towards financial decisions, but decided to follow my instinct. "Do not underestimate your instincts, child," Brahma had said kindly. "But understand to differentiate between your instincts and impulse. When it comes to money, patience is a bigger asset than many realize." These qualities seemed fairly probable and practical to exercise, once broken down into such simplicity and the fact that they could have such a long term impact on the enterprise made me wonder at the power of the basics in building and running a startup. While these thoughts circulated in my continuously expanding horizon, the last few words of Lord Brahma nailed the ultimate truth into my intellect. "There will be times when mistakes will take you off your course. There will be occasions when you will have come very far only to realize that you have chosen the wrong road, or that the road you had chosen suddenly gave in to circumstantial disruptions; all of this is expected," he explained. However, all large and mighty things come with an awareness and humility that keeps them grounded. "It is your strength to be humble. Remember that it is never late to admit that you have been wrong and never too late to change your course and return to home ground to start afresh." Many startups have begun making investments only to realize later that they had miscalculated their design. The wisest thing to do is to contract with minimum damage and look at the next best approach instead of continuing to ride a sinking ship.

With all these points put on the table, I was transported once again to my childhood memory of the Lakshmi Puja. I could see clearly that the presence of Devi Saraswati and Mother Parvati were imperative for the presence of Devi Lakshmi in any space. I had ignored this power and wisdom and set blindly with the vision of wealth in my mind. As the lessons of the day concluded, I came out better informed and a lot less intimidated by financial management. I knew that money treats you the way you treat it, coming back in the full circle of life and business.

Moral – Prudence is the key in planning expenditures based on priorities in your startup. A close assessment of the market trends, experiences of both, successes and failures of financial models of similar products in the market will bring you an insight that cannot be generated instinctively. In the matters of financial planning, it is advisable to start small, analyze the reactions in your environment and accordingly scale up or retract wherever deemed necessary. When it comes to finances, one should neither shy away from seeking mentorship nor from making mistakes, however to learn and admit one's faults and to change course as soon as this is identified is a wise approach to prevent larger losses.

9

The End of an Enterprise: Learnings from all failures

Long time ago, the soil of Indian earth was enraged with the biggest wars of all times. Many say that was a war for lands, some say it was intended as revenge. Some schools of thought also declare it as a power play, intended for bigger life lessons to be learned by the mortals. This was the war of Kurukshetra – the Mahabharata. Many allies joined hands for it, many parted ways, some in the name of power, some for dharma. Gods chose sides, so did nature. The legendary battle even induced interest in Kailash Parbat. People chose teams, onlookers watched in delight or horror, depending on what was going on and which side they had chosen to stand for. Shiva and Parvati did not come out in the open to act directly on sides, but their dharma and blessings found their way in the various channels to support sides that deserved their favour. All in all, it was a massive and strong act of men and gods, with many lessons to learn and teach. In the bigger war that went on for eighteen days, there were many small, yet significant battles fought on either side. Each of them had consequential roles to play and all inadvertently had many lessons to teach.

The reason I am telling you this is because I found one such battle extremely relevant to my situation at the moment. Shrishti had been started with highest of aspirations and had me under the illusion that it will turn into something big – a revolution in the travel industry with virtual reality. In the battle of Kurukshetra, Arjun was the star archer and warrior. He fought for the good and he fought well. But this incidence is not about Arjun. It is rather about his son, Abhimanyu. Now Abhimanyu was bright, intelligent and strong. Legend goes that he had learned the craft of forming and breaking through a Chakravyuh (a very special attack line in war field) from his father while still in his mother's womb. However, Arjun could not finish teaching him the entire formation. Abhimanyu's folly was that despite the lack of complete knowledge, he still went ahead and tried breaking the Chakravyuh formation; that caused a lot of confusion in the battle ground for his troops and eventually led to his death.

My case was not so severe; nobody was dying. But the principle of incomplete knowledge leading to self-destruction held out loud and clear. With my brain child, Shrishti, the knowledge had been effective, efficient but embarrassingly incomplete. This realisation, unfortunately, had not come to us in the beginning. Unlike Abhimanyu, who was aware of his folly and dared to take his chances anyway, I had been immersed in my own ego and had no clue about the disaster I was sailing proudly into. The results were laid out to me only when it was too late, that too by someone else who I had to hire, spending a lot of money!

"Not only does it hurt to have your skin ripped off, but what makes it worse is actually watching it done to you by someone who has paid for these services!" Chintan had exclaimed at the conclusion of the previous day's setting. I understood the pain of it and yet, the dark humour was not lost on me. My experience from all the previous sessions with Karma and Co had elevated from anger to astonishment, from frustration to understanding and from mistakes to learnings. With these set of learnings in mind, I had begun to realize the curve of failure, or as I would optimistically like to call it, experience with my startup. As I headed into the last session of the analysis and debriefing with my team, I couldn't decide whether I felt foolish for having lost, or wise for having learned. Only time would bring me to a conclusion.

Speaking of time, one of the most consistent observations I had made about Brahma was his respect for time. No matter what the assignment was, what the deadline of the task was or who it was that Brahma had committed his time to, he always maintained the discipline and respect for time I have never seen anyone else observe. Is that why he managed to control the perfect birth timings and schedules of all geneses across eras, millenniums or even seconds?

"I thought he'd have some extensive time management mechanism and equipment to help his with the multi universe time tables," Srijan had exclaimed.

"Are you telling me that all of that is installed only in his head?" I was in awe too. If nothing else, this would be my takeaway from Brahma – his immense regard for time and its optimum utilization. Starting that day, I started to time each of my activity, mental or physical, and reached the office exactly on time for the last session of the meeting.

Brahma had been helping us with a step by step walk through of gap assessment that had led Shrishti to its current situation. We had launched our brand, worked extensively on the marketing, convinced one of the biggest venture capitalist to give us seed funding and rocked the media space creating a buzz across all galaxies. We had brought on-board a team of extremely hard working and diverse set of interns and a manager with experience and loyalty that is hard to match even across the Swarga Lok. And yet, we had exhausted all our funding, failed to close a single deal with any client, even on earth and we stood at the brink of a shut down. We had been shocked, confused and disappointed with these mishaps. It was Brahma who had then opened our eyes with his enlightenment and showed us the various levels of our folly, hubris and naivety that had brought us to that.

"As we move into our last session for debriefing, I want you to understand that failures of startups are extremely common in the current scenario," Brahma began his carefully chosen words. "It is not the same as running traditional businesses anymore. You do not have that level of financial comfort, nor do you have the established footprint to validate your product." It is both a challenge and an opportunity to experiment. Although, it is risky with the hit and miss principle, if you can tap into a market scope with your beta product, you can set foundations or a promising empire. This, I had learned from the emphasis Brahma had laid on testing your product for market response before diving head first into business. "Do you have any idea how many models of Swarga Lok have been built and rebuilt to be able to fit the revolving population and rising standards of the place? A new successor walks in each time with an idea and the infrastructure has to be accommodating enough to make the changes and yet keep the core as consistent." I got the point. What I didn't get was how such decisions were to be made without putting everything at stake. As usual, he had answers to my questions even before I had worded them. As the roof once again turned into a constellation display, Brahmadoot moved the sky towards the lunar space, showing us the earth's sky at night with the full moon shining. "Chandra Dev has been the king of the night for ages. Just like Surya Dev has been our life giver for the day." Miraculously, the sky changed to day as Surya Dev showed up beaming his benign rays on all plants and animals of the planet. Both the gods have been dwelling in coexistence for many eras. But as Brahma explained, this was not the case once. Thousands of years ago, burning in their ambitions and blinded by their egos, both the gods got into a war of trying to conquer each other's space. "I can easily outshine the moon even at night," the Sun god had proudly proclaimed. "The Sun is only an arrogant burner while I am a soothing source of peace," Chandra Dev had retaliated. In the process of outdoing each other, they had started battling for longer days and nights respectively, making matters worse for the rest of the world. It was then that the universal manager, Lord Vishnu, had offered them to switch roles for a while to see how they felt about each other's power. Somewhat impressed, the sun took over the night and the moon went into the day. Hell broke loose at this turmoil! While the days became dim and lifeless, rendering everyone weak and helpless, the nights became scorching hot and too bright for anyone to sleep. Instead of being the gods they wanted to be, both the sun and the moon became a matter of curse for earthlings and joke for the celestials. "Do you know why that happened?" was the question popped at me. I thought they did not know how to control their powers. That wasn't it. Both Surya and Chandra had been doing their jobs for hundreds of thousands of years and knew exactly what they had to do to make the day and night function perfectly, in their respective domains. What they did not know, was how to handle what was beyond their expertise. "This is a common mistake that founders make with their startups. They get excited by an idea, try to implement their own skill sets in the said domain and completely ignore their lack of experience or knowledge in that area." As Brahma continued to explain this point, Chintan complained about the amplitude of our expertise in VR. He obviously wasn't seeing the point. We had expertise in VR, but not in the domain of travel services. Imagine Brahma hired contractors who made the planets to make the animals. Or if Mother Ganga, just because she is a water body, decides to settle a water body in Mars! She couldn't possibly do that without a geologist or ecologist, right? We knew all about virtual reality and could form any model, if resources permitted. But we couldn't claim ourselves to be the experts of the domain we are targeting. Do you know how many startups in India alone die every month without ever even reaching the funding stage, simply because they had no subject knowledge and expertise?

"There are three ways of approaching this problem," Brahma began to elucidate, "To adhere, to acquire or to associate." To adhere would typically mean to stick to your area of expertise and probe through the scope in the market for a unique idea. This is safe and allows for a confidence that is much needed in crossing the initial hurdles that come in the path of all founders. The second path would be to acquire the skill set through first-hand experience in the domain. The greatest chefs have worked under someone else to understand the intricacies of running a restaurant before opening their own business. Even among us celestials, the concept of avatars is closely associated with gods taking birth in some or the other form on a planet, especially earth, to understand the circumstances as first-hand witnesses and to make judgments for the future accordingly. The last path, Brahma explained, was that of association. You club your knowledge of back end with someone's knowledge of the front end or the other way around. This way, the synthesis is a genius, covering all aspects of your business. This allows for holistic and diverse understanding of the universe you are treading into, contributes to objective opinions and decisions and simply saves you from the risks of outsourcing your ideas to people or organizations you may have no control over. "There is a big 'if' here though," trust the god of enlightenment to cover all aspects! "You are risking partnership, most likely putting at stake a huge chunk of your brain child as co-sharing. This demands high levels of trust and compatibility." One needs to have an equal investment of passion and understanding to make an equation like this work. More often than not, such partnerships fall short of expectations, leading to the downfall of an otherwise promising enterprise. Clearly we had fallen short of any of the three routes, only counting on our back end skill to work for an industry we clearly had no experience about. *Point well taken.*

What had made matters worse for us was that while lacking in the industry knowledge had crippled our perspective from the outside, our lack of focus in approach and development had been slowly demolishing us from the inside. "You know how a little child sits down with a piece of paper to draw, with many colours and craft tools?" I could picture one of the baby humans sitting enchanted in front of his canvas and drawing everything that came to his mind, from hills to cars, flowers to food, and animals to fireworks. "There is obviously no coherence in such hard work, however beautiful the creation maybe." Irrespective of how attractive each aspect, feature or branching out in your startup may seem, it is important to stay focused on what it is that you had set out to do. There is a reason why age-old organizations clearly defined their mission and vision, carefully penned down their key objectives. Every so often, no ideas might spring into someone's head that may seem tempting and promising. The next thing you know, your organization has diversified into that highly promising and yet highly consuming wing which may later turn into a high maintenance segment. It is extremely important to keep revisiting the primary objective with which one had set out to start the entrepreneurial journey and to keep setting filters on what is a boon and what a bane in this path. It was all so relatable. We had wanted to revolutionize the travel industry. Instead, we had ended up setting up flamboyant models of the travel experiences, focused unrealistically on marketing ourselves as a brand that frankly did not even exist yet. With these disastrous mistakes, how did we ever imagine to succeed?

Now that all our truths had been laid bare in front of us, I had one news to hear. Was Shrishti still in a position to recover and save its name or had we long crossed the resurrection mark? I have to admit, in either case, I was ready to embrace the consequences. There was a sudden hush outside the door and in surprise, I watched Shiva, my father, my mentor, and Parvati, my mother, walk into the chamber as everybody, including Brahma stood up in reverence. Amidst all the whispering questions, I suddenly realized why he was here. Shiva, the destroyer, was the decider of fate for those whose journeys came to an end. However, unlike mortals, who looked at destruction as an inauspicious end, we celestials looked upon demolition as pious and generous because it paved way for something new, something beautiful to replace the old and archaic. He had been especially called by Brahma to break the news.

Lord Shiva didn't take long to hit the last nail in the coffin. "I can't say it is too late for you to mend your ways and revive because there is no scope of corrective measures in your situation. Unfortunately, your capital is spent, your business stands at a dead end and as it turns out, there is no mine to dig through to save what remains of Shrishti. In my opinion, it is time to end this and start afresh." With those words, he slashed out the name and documents of Shrishti and chopped off my name from the documents, thus seizing any identity I had with Shrishti. I wish I could say it didn't hurt. I had brought myself mentally prepared for this verdict. I had stood honest to my roles and responsibilities and stood guard to protecting my passion at all costs. And yet, it felt like my dream was being beheaded by Shiva because it failed to live up to the expectations it had been set against.

At this instance, I felt mother Parvati's hands on my shoulder, with strength to pull me through this ordeal. It was here that she turned to the mighty Shiva and said something to him. Both my parents turned lovingly at me and patted the back of my head, almost molding it with strength and dignity, despite my loss. The failure of Shrishti hurt, and yet, I felt like a bigger person, with more learnings, experiences and strength on my shoulders than any success or victory could have brought me. Mindful of all the hubris, all the assumptions I had made so far. With my ears grown to new power, I could hear the echo of all the wrong decisions I had made one after another. With my nose expanding into a giant and strong trunk, I became aware with heightened sense of all the risks I had put my team and well-wishers into. But I felt wise, wise like an elephant rising above all to see the truth from an objective point of view. With the ending of this session, I officially signed the closing of Shrishti using a chunk of my tusk, as a tribute to the mistakes made and lessons learnt. I could have left defeated and lost, but as I walked out the Brahma Lok, I found myself even more determined to make the best of this opportunity. I had been blessed by the mightiest and tamed by the best. With the closure drawn from the auspicious hands of Shiva, I knew that this end would only lead to the beginning of something better. I had to be mindful of all the points of learnings I had made and make the best of a second chance. I knew the path would not be easy and that I would be reminded, time and again of my folly and failure. And yet, I stood tall and strong, walking out as the real Ganesha – the elephant headed, as I had been destined to be, awaiting the new and exciting adventures I would begin here on.

Moral – *Failure in a startup is a predictable pattern, formed by the common mistakes of assumptions. These could be based on the working beyond your expertise and hoping things would work out, straying from the point of focus you had set out to accomplish with your enterprise, or simply, setting to work with a wrong set of people. A deep respect for resources made available to you is a must when hoping to run an enterprise. Similarly, a deep respect for the ultimate user of your product is the only fuel that will take you a long way with your endeavours. Actual failure is not in making mistakes, but in not realizing when a mistake has been made and retracing your steps to correct the errors. Never be afraid from starting anew, because that may be a blessing in disguise.*

10

No Space for Love:
the entrepreneurial compromises

*O*ur history, that the humans today call mythology, is full of stories of love and the victories based on love. Some couples and their stories have become eternal enough to inspire many, and yet, their true and real meaning may have been ignored in the material understanding of love. The biggest examples before us have been those of Lord Ram and Devi Sita and the beloved couple of Radha and Krishna. While the former were known for their wisdom, ideologies and deep understanding of one another, the latter were a symbol of uninterrupted and self-less devotion. It is said that Devi Sita was brought into the human world to bring awareness to Ram of his own powers, so that he could eventually overcome the evil. However, the story of Krishna and Radha gives an altogether different meaning to love. Mother Parvati would narrate stories to me about how Radha would wait endlessly for Krishna and give up everything for his love and attention. "That is love, Ganesha," mother would speak with overwhelming emotions in her eyes. "When you do not care about anything for yourself, nothing but the one you love." I knew she was teaching me in reference to sharing everything I won with Karthikey, my brother, but I also had begun to realize that when I grew up, I would understand and perhaps experience this emotion of devotion as shared by Radha-Krishna.

It is said that the two could not be told apart from one another, such was the greatness of their love. "But that is because Radha was a manifestation of Krishna himself…" Nandi Uncle had explained during our evening walks when I had shared my observations of love between the said couple with him. "Krishna discovered his inner elements and found out what his true inclination was because of the devotion of Radha. This is what the bigger meaning of love is. It is born from within and takes you through a journey inside out… showing you that there is no other."

I had known my enterprise to be my love, passion and I had dedicated my hard work, my energy and my dreams to it. However, everything had fallen apart within moments as I had been made to realize by the research and analysis done by Lord Brahma and I had been humbled into realizing all my faults. When they say love is blind, I had not realized that this blindness could convolute into one's passion and dreams in life and lead to its very downfall. I had been too blindly in love with my brain child to notice and evaluate its faults and thus, met with its end in the dust.

Mulling over these thoughts in my head, I walked into the Indian subcontinent and began marching past the valleys where father used to take me to show the various shades of humankind.

Eventually, I came across the banks of river Ganga and found myself sitting at the ghat, dwelling over life, of my existence and of the course I would take up next and whether at all, I had control over how things would flow from here on. It was then that I felt a glow of warmth drifting towards me. It almost felt like a shining piece of gold floating onwards, and against the reflection of the setting sun, all I could see were the glistening edges of this being. As the figure got closer and closer, I realized that it was a woman, so delicate and radiant in being that her shine was both difficult and irresistible to look at. Finding myself in this sudden trench of a mysterious aura, I waited impatiently as she approached me and greeted me with kind words.

"Pardon me, O beautiful eyed king, but I could not help but notice how much strength and yet how much gentleness you radiate in your being," she spoke in delightful shyness. I was immediately taken aback by this statement for it was I who had been struck by her enlightened features. Introducing herself as Tulsi, the enigmatic lady sat close by and started talking to me about the river Ganga and her ephemeral beauty. "This very same Ganga starts as a small trickle off the glacier, takes the form of powerful falls down the mountains, transforms into a generous abundance at the plains or floods with all her might before melting formlessly into the ginormous ocean!" She reflected in awe, "There are so many forms and qualities in us, Ganesha, that we may not have even discovered yet, but they are all lying within us, waiting to be explored." I felt a certain epiphany in that moment that I was there for a purpose and that Tulsi had appeared at that very ghat in that very instance also for a purpose. This opened an entirely new dimension of thoughts in my head and got me ready to explore whatever lay ahead with an open heart and mind. I opened my heart out to the kind and gentle Tulsi and revealed to her about all my struggle, my defeat, my current state of mind as I felt lost, discouraged and confused about the next course of actions. She listened to me patiently and nodded with understanding and acceptance where I sought it. What I most particularly noticed was that even though my own follies were evident as was my lack of wisdom, never once during the entire narration of my tale did I see a sign of judgments being made or emotions being dismissed at her end. Tulsi listened kindly but also wisely. She asked questions where information was necessary and nudged me to carry on from parts where she thought brooding was unnecessary. "Do you know what hurt the most?" I asked rhetorically, "That it was me all along... I had been the one making each and every decision, thus sharpening the sword for my own beheading!" She nodded as though she understood as I poured out my worst realizations, my most honest confessions that I had not even shared with Chintan and Srijan on our way back from the last session of debriefing at the Karma office. Why was I being so honest and free with Tulsi? I had no idea. Was it because at that moment, I needed someone to hear me out, to unburden me of all my pain? Or was it because she was a perfect stranger that I had no risks of sharing my deepest and most heartfelt emotions with? Whatever it was, I knew that I could not have found a better audience, nay a participant to balm my pains and calm my nerves.

Through our conversations, I noticed one thing in particular. Every question that Tulsi asked me struck me particularly with two elements. Firstly, she talked to me as though she knew me really well and understood my flow of thoughts as if she were inside my head. The second peculiar thing about her conversations was that all her questions or responses steered towards solutions or constructive reasoning. Not once did she ask me about why I had done what I had done or what and how had I lost what I had lost. While she let me vent out all pent up frustrations, she never once stopped to brood over them, as though they were dust on the shoulders, meant to be brushed off to move on.

"So, Ganesha, now that your heart is completely free of any boundaries, which way do you want to head now?" I had honestly never thought of my 'big loss' as that. She brought a new perspective to my large ears then. "When your hands empty off one karma, it means you are ready to fill them up with something else now. You obviously cannot grasp new things in life if your hands are already full with your past, can you?" Oh! That simple statement, that child-like innocence of a question, all of this rang so many bells in my mind. It was as though Ganga herself was splashing sense back into me with her generous waves. With Tulsi's exclamations twirling in front of my mind, I began to realize that this indeed was an opportunity for me, with all my learnings, to start afresh towards a goal that could fill my heart.

But which way was I to go? I had no idea. Ever since I had found the courage to think about building my own enterprise, Shrishti, travel agency and virtual reality were all the colours that occupied my spectrum of thoughts! How could I start walking in any one direction with enough confidence to feel that it would not be the wrong path to choose? I expressed my panic to Tulsi, since we were being completely honest and I could see that expressing what was within would at least make me feel better and not worse.

"Alright, let us not think so ahead of ourselves and break the roads that we haven't even chosen, let alone walked on already!" She joked to lighten the mood. "If there was any one thing that would cheer you up, no matter what was going wrong, what would it be?" she enquired.

"Food… a nice, warm laddu, to be specific," I replied instantly. I had no doubt about that. This was an inside joke at the Kailash Parbat too. Whenever I got upset because of a scolding from Father Shiva or a fight against Kartikey, mother would simply put a plate full of laddus at the doorstep of my room. Next thing they know, I am chirping around, playing with my rat or teasing Nandi Uncle for something or another. Food was my happy spot!

"Great then, let us get you some food, Ganesha," she beamed as though she was happy just in my happiness.

We went and found some laddus and I sat satiated, just looking in awe at the magical influence they had on my mood and composure. After consuming the first few bites in stunning silence, I let out a sigh of satisfaction and blurted, "If there's anything that truly holds my passion, apart from Ma and Baba, it is food." I had not finished the sentence when I noticed Tulsi's eyes widening in excitement, as though she had stumbled upon a treasure that was sitting right under her nose. Clueless of what she was going so bubbly about, I asked with my questioning eyes, since my mouth was still stuffed with the last bite of another soft laddu. She indicated excitedly to the laddu and then to me. It took me a few minutes to gulp down the sweetness and ask out loud, "Are you thinking what I think you are thinking?" It was an obvious indication towards me and my connection with food. All the while being lost and discouraged, I had been turning to food for solace and that was exactly what I had forgotten to notice. Food is what drives me. I will fight any battle, move any mountain and burn the midnight lamp for a laddu, especially one made by mother Parvati. This is what my true passion is. I nodded in complete agreement with Tulsi and we sat down to discuss the various ideas that could lead my way with food. I had to keep in mind to think of a product and idea relative to my target audience and then make a realistic start, unlike the previous attempt, which had been a shot in thin air. So I began internal deliberation and kept blurting things out in front of Tulsi. "Why do I turn to food?" That was because it was comforting and when everything in the world was going wrong, I wanted something as comforting as homemade food to calm me down and make me feel like I am in my mother's arms again. So what could we do with that? Could we come up with a food delivery system? But that would be just a scoop of the cream; I needed to dig deeper. Could I start an entire enterprise based on comfort food, with a feeling of homemade style, one that would be made available in a way that everyone can relish it as though they are eating in their childhood home?

"Maybe you can bring more diversity in this and make your service customizable?" I heard a somewhat distant voice of Tulsi amidst the clouds of my thoughts. I had almost forgotten about her sitting there by my side because my excitement and deliberation had taken me far away from that ghat into my own mental version of virtual reality. With her voice in my consciousness, I realized I should make myself present with her and I did. I turned to her and tried asking more about her opinion on this issue.

"I do not know much about business, Ganesha, you are a better judge of things, but I can say this much that whatever you devise, you must ensure that it attracts people for what value or sentiment you are trying to sell and not the outer shell of how you are selling it. Otherwise, it will just turn into another glamorous hat that people come to look at but no one wants to wear." I heard her and found my thoughts drifting away again towards Shrishti and to the fact that this is exactly what had gone wrong with the enterprise. I would need to be very conscious of what I am selling. I felt my mind settling down now after the initial excitement of the idea and I decided to get in touch with Srijan and Chintan to discuss with my creative as well as logical intellect about the next steps of action.

And yet again, I was gone, far away in my thoughts from Tulsi, forgetting that I needed to at least respect her with my presence because it was she who had brought me into a languid discussion and helped me relieve myself of the stress of the past, she who had helped me speak my heart and mind and rebuilt my confidence, she who had nudged me towards a new idea, towards my true love (which I would have missed out on if not for her wise observation) and yet, she sat right next to me and she had been completely forgotten. If these weren't enough signs to pay heed to, what happened next was a clear flag for my mind. Seeing me back to the consciousness of the present, Tulsi looked at me lovingly and asked, "Dear Ganesha, now that you are here, I would like you to know that from the instance you walked on to this ghat, you had my attention and with it my heart. It is your honesty that moves me and your dedication towards your dreams that makes me want to follow you and stand with you through your journey. In return, I ask for nothing but your love." The overwhelming burden and guilt that these words of the kind Tulsi filled me up with is unfathomable. It was a clear sign for me that I was not made for such a bond.

With as much gentleness as possible, I replied, "Dear kind and wise Tulsi, you have brought to me an entire era of thoughtfulness and consideration that I had been lacking all this while. You have lent your kind ear and heart to me and relieved me of all my anxiety and inspired me to look in the upward direction. I am much in gratitude to you and in awe with your wisdom." However, as I saw her smile with a blush, I corrected my praises immediately lest they lead to a miscommunication, "But, dear lady, I am bound by dharma and drive only to my parents and to my devotion towards creating something of my own. Within the last few hours of our encounter, I have found so often my mind wandering into the new ideas that you have nudged at me and all this time, I had forgotten of your mere presence!" With every word I said, I knew I was making matters worse for her.

"But, I have been the one helping you out in the process of rediscovery, haven't I?" She questioned almost pleading.

"You are right, it was you who brought me out of my own dilemma and you were the objective outlook that I needed to break from my own block." I answered in earnest.

"I do this because I love you and I know that I can be your aid. All I ask in return is for you to reciprocate the love and let me be your companion."

It is not that the idea of companionship had not occurred to me before this. There were times, especially when in triumph or in defeat, when I felt the need to share my experience with someone and have someone to fall back on. However, I was extremely aware of the repercussions that such companionship came with. It would mean that I would have to share responsibility at both professional as well as personal front. It would mean emotional commitment to do enough justice to my partner and more than anything else, it would mean distraction from my priority. At this early stage of my entrepreneurial journey, when I was still finding my own footsteps, I could not afford to support someone else walk with me and have us both become burdens on each other. I continued trying to explain to Tulsi my emotional dilemma.

"There are priorities in my mind that cannot afford being diverted from. I understand that companionship is important and I am no exception in wanting it. But I know that it will come with prices I cannot afford to pay right now."

Pained with rejection, she exclaimed, "But what do I lack? What do you want that is missing in me? I could be everything you want me to." I was stuck on trying to explain to her the classic, 'it is not you, it is me'- logic.

"The timing is not right, Tulsi. Had I met you a couple of years ago, this would have worked or perhaps, a couple of years from now, when my feet have found a landing in the entrepreneurial kingdom, this would work out just fine. But with all my heart and mind, I know that my dedication belongs with building my business."

I apologized profusely to the magnificent woman before me, asking for leave from her heart as I could not bear to give her pain. "I am not one for ties. I will not be able to do you any justice, nor will I feel free enough to follow my drives if I am tied to your obligation. Pardon me, sweet kindness, for I take your leave, but I will forever be obliged for the kindness you have rendered upon me."

She left me with words that would probably haunt me for a very long time, for I knew not and at least feared that they may be true, "I will let you go Ganesha, but know that when you have everything you call your passion and dream, and find no one on your side to share it all with, you will turn back and look at this day and think of me."

I could not bear to turn back as I left the ghat that very instance. I knew I had left behind a broken heart and multitude of tears for Tulsi to nurse. I felt malignant and yet my sense of justice advised me that in the long run, this would be the right thing to do, instead of raising her hopes for a life she could not have. Were Tulsi's words true? Would I have to end up alone because of the entrepreneurial journey I had pledged to embark upon? I could not answer for sure. But I knew that in that instance, I felt like I had made the right call. At every stage of life, priorities differ and so do our decisions based on them. I could not fathom making enough space in my life to attend to someone in a personal space. Building an enterprise is not an easy process and requires a lot more diligence than appears. There are difficult choices to face and sacrifices to make. Once I had my mind set on something, I knew I would have to stick to it with all my strength.

With heaviness and nervousness, I walked to the entry of Kailash Parbat where, in the distance, I could see Chintan and Srijan waiting. I walked with my hopes raised now, with determination that things were going to change for the good, for the food!

Moral – An entrepreneur's journey is not an easy one. There are dead ends, compromises, sacrifices and dilemmas that change how we perceive our world. The solution only lies in looking deep within to understand what we love and then in following that with no deviation. The prices to pay will be high sometimes, but in the long run, it is better to keep priorities straight and simple; only this way will we be able to win the bigger battle.

11

Food for Thought: Ganesha explores the food industry

*T*he idea of incubation comes with passion and realization that you have to work in an area that you have at least some idea about. I had been passionate about food since childhood. After having my attention drawn towards it during my interaction with Tulsi, my next steps were to explore the gaps in the food industry and understand how I could introduce virtual reality in a space with innovative means. This time around, I was determined to keep a strong administration on all my research and homework before diving head first into all the expenditure at the thought of whatever looks attractive. It had so far been a steady and yet painfully slow process to exercise patience and wisdom to not jump at the first idea, first option or first opinion that came in the jurisdiction of the food industry. I have decided to pen down all the ideas that occur to me as opportunity related to startup ideas for the food industry. And then, I will rationalize for and against each of these aspects to reasonably conclude to the best option out of these. From the position of purchasing of raw material for production of food article, to its manufacturing process, from its marketing and branding to selling, from advertisement to storage and ultimately, the supply to the final user, the food industry involves several processes. There is sufficiency and efficiency at all levels, but this is what can be termed as an insatiable industry because of being subject to continuous consumption. Anything in the world of business that is consumed as a continuous process is always in need for innovation and improvement because the consumer is easily bored with the monotony of consumption. It is because of this very reason that anything food related always has scope for innovation and addition to an otherwise efficient system in its current state.

It is with this insight that I decided to study all levels of the 'food chain'. "Mother Parvati, give me leave to wander around the entire creation. I will explore all the worlds that eat and find out what works and what is missing."

Parvati gave her beloved son her blessings with a knowing smile. After all, she knew about my love for food. "Ganesha has a gift for understanding food. He can tell by the mere smell of a cuisine about what ingredients have been used and in what quantity," she would often talk affectionately, "He also knows where you will find the best of all varieties of indigenous food items; he really knows about all this."

"Where do you think I should begin this quest, mother? Where will I find the most insight about the food industry?" I asked mother Parvati.

"My child, the universe has varied relationship with food. For some, it is a matter of survival, while for some, it is a source to earn a living. Some use food for connections and some for revenge. Food is both an offering and a gift, a blessing and a praise, all camouflaged with sentiments for those associated with it. There will be different perspectives from every person you speak to!" Parvati's words were magical to my creative mind.

My head started bustling with all these opportunities I could explore. "Calm down, Ganesha!" I had to check myself, "Let us not get ahead of ourselves once again. This time, make up your mind only when you have done your homework." With this food for thought, I soared into the *Vayumandal*, with my pet rat to meet different people.

The first on this journey was Shri Krishna, sitting by the sunset, watching the human world preparing to go back to their homes for a night's rest. "Greetings, Krishna!" I folded my hands in a respectful namaste as Krishna smiled at me.

"Greetings, dear Ganesha. What brings you out of Kailash, into the open grounds?"

I liked Krishna; he always spoke intelligently and came directly to the point, aware and practical. "Krishna, I am trying to research about what different people think and need about the food they eat or is available to them. I certainly know you like eating too! Would you tell me about your thoughts on this?"

Krishna, always up for a good and interesting conversation went on to explain about his favourite cuisine, the homemade butter. "You know Ganesha, just one spoon full of that butter is enough to make everything else on the plate taste amazing. But the only problem is that despite knowing the recipe, I have never been able to find the same flavour that I used to eat in Vrindavan, where all the mothers would sit together and make the butter. What would I do to taste that flavour again!" I noted this interesting perspective and thanked Krishna for his time. This was a good start, but I wanted more assessment. So I went to Visnhu's abode to figure how the management giant felt about food and its availability. "Even the big shots must eat, right?" I thought to myself as I nervously entered the head office.

"Greetings, dear Ganesha." Vishnu embraced me with warmth, "Your father Shiva had already called me to inform about your visit." I couldn't help but smile to myself. It is always a good lesson to learn from father on how to manage relations, and how to secure yourself a good ear when meeting someone big.

"Never shy away from using your resources, Ganesha. They will come handy in more ways than you can imagine," Father Shiva had advised me as a parting gift for this journey. Clearly, his experience had brought him the foresight to make things easier for me in my research. With this consideration in my mind, Ganesha dived directly into the questions, owing to the busy schedule of Vishnu. "You have such a large enterprise to deal with, and like all good machinery, even your human resource surely need food for good performance. So how do you handle availability, choices or even basic procurement when you have to organize events or when someone is visiting?"

Vishnu's troubled face revealed that a nerve had been hit. There was clearly some trouble in this diocese that the great manager had not been able to resolve. "Management at this scale is chaotic. Right now, we just call in caterers and ask to cook what the majority generally likes. I know this does not make everyone happy, but honestly, who has the time and energy to go into micro-management? If I had something on my fingertips, which I could just brief my hospitality department with. I am sure, we would have a more organized and efficient way of providing people with food that they want and yet without the hassles!" I nodded. This was an expected issue. Food is a personal choice and customization is critical. However, nobody has the time to pick and scan through the extensive menus that restaurants offer, especially when they want orders in bulk. I could feel myself being subjected to new challenges and perspectives; this was definitely a good idea.

Taking leave from Vishnu, I had just about begun stepping into the earth's atmosphere when I stumbled upon Narada who was coming back from his trip to the *bhu-lok* or favouritely known as earth. "Narayan, Narayan, what is Ganesha, the wise soul from Kailash Parbat, doing so far away from home?" Narad, as always, asked with his spicy inquisition.

"Narad Muni ji, Pranaam," I bowed respectfully. "I am so glad I ran into you. I am travelling around the universe in search of some answers related to food."

Narada's eyes brightened up at the name of food and he blurted excitedly, "Oh, I just had the universe's best jalebis before leaving for *par-lok*. I wanted to bring some with me, but they are not easy to carry, you know!" This was a new perspective that attracted my attention immediately. "So if there was a way of getting your favourite cuisine transported to you, would you be willing to pay for that?"

Narad's excited smile was enough to convey the answer, "Oh, you name a price, my son! Do you have any idea how many planets and galaxies I travel around every year? Each place has its unique cuisine and although when visiting I get to eat a lot, when I am back, I miss those flavours. If I could get them transported to me, it would be a miracle!"

With each interview, I continued to find more and more evidence that people needed specific kind of availability with food. Clearly, these needs has not been met by the market yet.

Bidding good bye to Narada, I headed to earth, to meet my favourite Guru Vashishtha who was working on a ginormous ritual of feeding a thousand brahmins. "Namaste, Guru Vashishta, it is so good to see you after long!"

Vashishtha was pleased to meet me after all these years too. I seemed to have impressed many people, with all my wisdom and with even as a child and Guru Vashishtha was also one of them. "To what do I owe this honour, Ganesha?"

Now, I knew, from experience that Guru Vashishtha was a proud man and would feel insulted if told that I was visiting just for research. In all these years, well taught by experience, I had mastered the art of speaking the language that my audience understands. "Guruji, I am always eager to learn and observe your rituals, you know that. And since you are feeding a thousand brahmins today, I thought I must not miss this opportunity to receive some of your blessings too!" I said, pointing at my large belly, always eager to eat.

It was after a hearty meal and a beautiful ceremony that I tactfully brought up the subject with the sage. "Guruji, preparation of such a large meal must be a task of huge responsibility, right? How do you manage?"

Vashishtha, clearly exhausted from his hard work, spoke candidly with me, "Oh you have no idea! The essence of the meal is its pure and clean ingredients. I cannot trust anyone with the quality, so I have to do most of this work myself. I can't tell you how exhausting such preparations are, especially at the frequency at which they are organized. What would I give to find someone who could take care of the quality of this service for me!" I knew this was a major concern, even in Kailash Parbat. Shiva often organized large scaled yajnas and it was mother Parvati who had to administer the preparations because quality was of the essence. Registering this thought into my notebook, I thanked Guru Vashishtha for his time and a hearty meal and headed to meet some common people of a city nearby.

"It would help to know what common people think about this subject," I thought to myself, heading towards a group of women resting in the courtyard. The women, clearly tired after a long day's work, were resting and catching up with each other as I approached them with hands respectfully joined together. "Ladies, namaste, can I bother you for a few minutes? I am doing some research on food and would love to hear your opinion."

The women smiled at each other as one answered, "Food is our daily job. From meals to *prasads*, from festival cuisines to nutritional diet, we make everything at home, with our own hands. What do you want to know?"

I was glad I had chosen to speak to such an appropriate target audience. "Would you prefer if you could get good food from outside, so that you don't have to work so hard?"

The women made faces and did not seem convinced by the idea. "There are many outlets that offer food. But why make our family eat outside food with undependable quality or too much oil and spices when we are experts in making what they want?

Anyway, when the husbands and children have to step out, they are forced to eat that outside food!"

This clicked an idea in my head and I jumped to ask. "And what if when you or your family is not at home, but they still get to eat home cooked food with the same quality and taste? Would you like that?"

The women stared at each other and smiled. "Why not? That would reduce half our tension by simply giving the right food to our family!" I smiled and thanked them extensively. After a little bit of chit-chat about their local flavours, I took my leave and continued on my journey.

Thus, I went around meeting people from all sorts of backgrounds. I met the temple saints who said they would like their prasads to be delivered directly to the gods. I met the gods who said they'd like to have organized access to the offerings. I met travellers who said they'd like to see what food is available before they order. There were some who said they want only home cooked meals while some who said they were tired of the monotony of flavours. Some preferred healthy diets while some looked at how attractive their food was. I even met chefs and shop owners who wanted to spread their businesses across geographies, who already had demands but very little means to supply. I was also particular to notice that for those with simpler choices, cost of the food available was a major concern. While those who had specific and selective needs were willing to pay a price, as long as these demands were met. Through all these conversations from far and wide, it was clear that there was a clear need in the market of food industry. All I had to do now was chalk out this need, narrow down the map and see what product would be built out of it.

After days of travelling and research, I began missing home, and especially mother. With my little VR device, I called Ma to see what she was up to. "What are you doing, Ma?" I asked affectionately.

"Oh, Ganesha," Ma spoke back from her kitchen. "I know you are due back soon. So I am making your favourite modaks for when you come back!" I was overwhelmed to see mother's affectionate smile. As she brought the modak into the main frame, the VR device showed its contents, its temperature and even enlisted the nutritional qualities of the modak. I had made this device for mother Parvati to help her in her purchases when she wanted to ensure that she was buying good quality products for her kitchen. "This seems to be working effectively to even show and display a food product," I thought in my head as the electric visuals of the food increased my appetite further for my favourite dessert!

With such thoughts and processes running in my head, I completed my journey of several days and returned to Kailash Parbat. It was now time to analyze the findings and discuss what ideas could be brought to the table with the team. I sat down with Chintan and Srijan as Ma brought me the favourite laddoos to eat. As I summarized the various research interviews, they made bullet points of the several take-aways from the discussions. Out of the many learnings, the main points deciphered were that:

1) Intergalactic transportation of food items was not available at a good scale.

2) Indigenous cuisines have a high demand, but barely any supply chain.
3) Quality of the food is essential.
4) People like customizable products that suit their need.
5) A hassle free system of easy food delivery is critically absent in the market.
6) A good visual of the food is extremely efficient in bringing customers to business.

There were several anecdotes attached to these points, but it was clear to the team that a delivery centric system could hit the market in a way that made available the most unique flavours across territories. In doing so, however, a standardized process and system to ensure quality and efficiency would be the key to operation and success of one such model. With these learnings in place, we sat down to determine what could the details of such a product be and how would it convert into a successful business model. "We need to focus on a certain demography that is willing to pay for good quality service. We cannot make a product that is good for all, otherwise, we lose our viability and practical scalability," Chintan added after thinking, "The price needs to be competitive with actual food stores, but replacing them with reliability and quality will bring us scale and ultimate revenue."

Things were beginning to sound reasonable. The idea was to build a model that could produce local and special cuisines as per instructions or simply reproduce specialty cuisines but under strong quality administration and have them delivered to desired destinations. We would scan the market for producers that are in demand, bring them on board with our brand, have them manufacture their specialty food items, but in the way we want it, and sell it with our carefully designed packaging and branding. People would be able to order with us online using our VR model, strategically available on all public portals on line and in stores, to view their product, understand its composition and order as per their need.

We would ensure to invest as little as possible in the beginning, working on the available resources of the food manufacturers that we tie up with. With very limited resources and people at hand, I decided to split the team and work on two stages simultaneously. While one would get down to speaking to potential clients and ask for their opinion on the product, the other would work on a beta version of the technology to test with the said clients, in order to gain insight and recommendations in the beginning of product development. I was determined to begin with a small pilot within Kailash to see how the implementation would work and to assess the plausible challenges with minimum possible damage. We simply could not afford monitory shocks at this stage. As I watched the team get back on the table and brainstorm about the possibilities, I took a step back and breathed nervously. I was reminded of these discussions and excitement that the team had encountered during Shrishti, the last enterprise that had failed miserably. Doubts and fear crept into my consciousness. But I was wiser and stronger with my learnings, "Not this time, we won't fail. One step at a time, we will build this process from the ground. This time, I am ready."

Moral – *The foundation of any building is begun by digging underground. So that, even before the building takes shape on the ground, the support has found its place beforehand. Building an enterprise is the same. Never, ever shy away from exploiting your connections and resources if they help you gain a better position in your transactions. Assessing the market needs helps you understand the gaps. But this assessment must come from multiple viewpoints. And once you have the analysis, it is best to get to the testing stage, at an affordable scale, instead of building theories on paper while you lose precious time. It is wise to assume nothing and go well-informed. As little pieces of information come together, you will find yourself better equipped to take baby steps towards your idea. Once your idea has found its strength, only then begin working on your product. Remember, the journey of a thousand miles begins with simple, small steps!*

12

The Enterprise Takes Forms:
the making of "Sweet Post"

There's a thing about something you are passionate about. You are willing to push your limits, try everything in your capacity to make your 'work' better and above all, crossing all boundaries about what you will and will not do to achieve what you have set out for. It doesn't matter if you are an engineer, a doctor, a management expert, a chef, an architect or a writer. When it comes to building your own enterprise, you become everything. You forget these labels and levels and you dive in head first to become whatever is needed of you. If you keep thinking about only what you have done so far or what in your head is your capability, then you get only so far. On the other hand, if you knock down these chains and own up to the nuts and bolts of your enterprise, not only do you get things done more concretely, but you have a hands on experience that motivates you to handle whatever may come your way on the path of success. I had learned this watching my father, Shiva. It didn't matter whether he was talking to the gods, the kings, the *aghoris* in his team or simply the common people. He became one with them, he worked at their level, shoulder to shoulder and there was nothing he wouldn't do. That is the trick of running a successful business or even a successful life. And in the course of my own entrepreneurial journey, I learned with first-hand experience that if I had a shot of being successful, I would have to do the same.

After having built the idea of the food enterprise that I had been researching on, it was time for me to start with a pilot. Chintan and Srijan, by now, had become efficient in designing the virtual reality model because of our previous venture. So I was assured that department was taken care of. And even though this is my favourite part and it makes me very happy sitting in a room and submerging myself with the design, I knew that I needed to focus on things that needed work from ground zero. Thus, I turned my attention to our product – food. It had been decided that I would try to club my idea with some local sweet producers and try to market our product. I went to speak with the most famous *halwai* (sweets producer) in Kailash. I don't know what I was expecting, but I learned a lot in this encounter.

"Hello, *kaka,* how are things cooking?" I started with small talk.

"It is going ok. The festive season starts only next month so we are a little relaxed at the moment. But the prices have gone up for milk, so I am finding it a little difficult to keep the profit margin intact. Hopefully, better sales next month will compensate for it." Kaka had been running the shop for over forty years. People came from all over to his shop just for a small pack of his sweets. All pilgrims usually stopped by too. In all the years that I had been around, I had never seen the shop shut or the taste of the sweets change. "I can understand kaka… but why don't you try some sweets that don't need milk. At least for the moment, that may help with the price, don't you think so?" Now, I know Kaka comes with a very traditional school of mind. He is not very fond of changes and does not agree to things easily. But I had a plan in mind and if he agreed, I would get an introduction to test my product.

"I don't know how to make sweets besides the ones I sell here. Other than that, it is too much hassle to start with something new all over. My customers like what I sell and I will stick to that."

This sounded like trouble to me. You can't change generations of consistency with a new idea with the wave of a wand. I had to be patient and realistic. "Kaka, there's a special sweet I have now been making for years. Many people who come to our house have had it and love the taste like anything. The interesting part is that it does not require milk in a large quantity, but tastes just as good. Would you like to try some of that and give me feedback?" I could sense the apprehension in his voice, but I think my polite behaviour and the offer to get his feedback convinced him to give it a try. I brought out the special modaks I had prepared in the morning and offered him a piece. I watched him closely as he observed the appearance, the smell and eventually the taste of what I believed to be great modaks by my standard.

"These taste great, Ganesha!" he said with a miserly smile. "But they look so different. I don't think people will like the way it looks." I understood his reaction. He had obviously a very set mindset about how his sweets looked and could not imagine anything out of the box.

"Would you like to do an experiment with me, Kaka? Would you like to sell some of these modaks and see what people think about it?" I was pushing my luck here, but I had nothing to lose.

"If they don't like it, it will ruin my reputation! Never in forty years has anyone walked out of this store without liking what they ate…" I had seen this coming. I would have to think of some other way to try but at this stage, I couldn't afford to anger him because I needed him to be on my side. I thanked him for his time and as I was just stepping out of the store with perplexities of what to do next, I saw a man standing on the opposite side of the street, selling umbrellas outside a store that sold rain boots. I turned out and ran back to Kaka with an idea bubbling in my head. Again, it was worth a shot and I wouldn't know if I didn't try. "Kaka, people won't have to walk out of your store unsatisfied. What if I could just showcase these modaks outside your store for a day? They don't have to associate it with your name, but if they like it, I will at least get a feedback. Just give me a chance?" By the looks on his face, I thought Kaka was about to lose his temper. Had I gone too far? But just as my fear started to boil, he smiled and gave up, "Alright. You're a good kid. Do what you like. But don't tell them these are sweets from my store. And don't pester people into buying them, ok?"

I practically ran back home to call Srijan. I had actually not expected this agreement, but now there was work to be done for the next day. He was over in a few minutes, updating me about the portal's work on VR. "We are running short of a few supplies,

Ganesha. Some things need to be bought for the design." I was beginning to dread that word like a child dreads Monday morning for school. We couldn't afford anything right now.

"We will make with what we have, Srijan," I explained. "Remember, this is a beta version and needs efficient working, not glossy looks." We needed to keep reminding each other from time to time about our previous failure with Shrishti. The game changing lesson from this disaster was to start small and solid. We couldn't afford any extravaganza anymore, since we were bootstrapping on this venture. With suggestions of some alternatives we could try and with ideas to recycle some of our materials remaining from Shrishti's VR equipment, we decided to continue.

"It will take a lot more time, Ganesha," Srijan added in the end. "So we will work day and night… but that is how it will be done," I replied knowing it was time to push some boundaries.

Switching back to the work ahead, I briefed him about my encounter with Kaka and how I planned to pitch my product in the market. Obviously, there were apprehensions. But I wasn't going to stop, not anymore. With diligent assistance from Srijan, we spent a few hours in the kitchen with the slow and steady process of making the modak. My own special twist included adding different agents for sweetness instead of regular sugar. Mother Parvati stood alongside the entire time, with tips and tricks for speeding up the process. "If you want the shape of the modaks to be more conventional, based on Kaka's reaction, you could make them into simple balls. But remember that this is your first chance to introduce the product in the market and people will choose it over other things only if it stands out," she advised.

She was right; this was our first and the most critical appearance in public and we needed it to be original. The rest of the evening was spent in careful monitoring of the modaks to ensure they stay in the right temperature and look presentable. Srijan and I sat with mother for hours into the night, joined by Chintan later with his head buzzing over restructuring the remains of Shrishti's equipment. We laughed all night over mother's story about my childhood. I would play different characters in a self-made game and talk to myself back and forth playing the king, the jester and the knight, all by myself. "Things haven't changed all that much, Ganesha..." she pointed out as I lay my tired head in her lap. I continued to play the childhood game in my head and built my resolution even stronger to become whatever it took to make this work.

It had been more than a couple of hours since I had been standing outside Kaka's store with modaks on display. I had to keep switching between the two boxes back and forth so that they did not dry up in the open. I had been drying my throat with continuously attracting people to try the modaks. I had decided not to charge any money at this stage and only look for feedback. To my surprise, even then, there had hardly been anyone interested in trying the modaks. It took a couple of hours before the regular customers walked into the store to buy their regular sweets and showed interest in trying some of my sweets. The reaction was, however, beyond satisfaction. They liked it, asked for more and even shared some with others around them. As the evening crowd took over, more and more people grabbed pieces off my boxes, but most left without questions or words of interest. By the time the store was closing up, I had only a couple of pieces left in my box with barely any feedback on the product. I offered my last piece to Kaka and waited for his response. "Some things don't work, no matter how hard you try, Ganesha. "He said sympathetically. You asked for a chance and I gave it to you, but now, you must let normalcy restore around my store, is that ok?" I nodded with polite gratitude at the chance he had given me and walked back home. I don't know what I had expected out of this day. But it was obviously a little unnerving to watch my hard work disappear without consequences. I was trying not to feel discouraged, but these little things do take a toll on you at some point of time.

Determined not to let it pull me down, I started the next day with a lot of energy, spent time cooking and chatting with my mother in the kitchen, asking her more and more about the colloquial food she had grown up with and building ideas on what else I could try. I was thus cooped between taking notes, researching on the internet and communicating with my team about the progress. In my heart, I was nervous, a little annoyed too, but at no point would I let this emotion spill over on those around me. I needed to keep the focus and energy high for the sake of everyone.

"Do you think people like changing their food habits frequently?" I was speaking to our cook, Vrinda, in the house to get more nuanced understanding.

"It depends, Ganesha, on what is the cause of this change. Sometimes, it is finances; at other times, it is influence with what is popular and available. But yes, people do change…" We heard a sudden bellowing at the door. Nandi Uncle, who is always guarding our entrance at his desk, came in with an excited look on his face to tell me that someone was eagerly looking for me at the door.

I saw Kaka pacing up and down the porch. "Ganesha, my boy, where have you been? The store is going crazy asking for those sweets you brought yesterday. Everyone thinks they were amazing and are coming back with orders for more!" I thought I was dreaming. "I was wrong, Ganesha. If you do try hard enough, you will get what you want, sooner or later." I was overwhelmed with his words and promised to get back to him as soon as possible. He had already been asked for more than twenty kilograms of modaks in all and I had no idea how I was going to work this out!

"Amma, this is a lot of expense… and we don't have that kind of resources here to produce that many sweets in this little time!" I confessed my anxiety to mother.

"May I suggest something?" Nandi Uncle spoke from a corner. His experience and insight was well known and respected in our family. "If I have to build a house, I will start at the ground, not in the factory. You want to sell sweets and you have a halwai for orders. Won't it make sense to use his kitchen and his people to make the sweets?" That was genius! I rushed to Kaka with everything I had at hand. He agreed willingly. I will give you some space and two of my people. We are done with today's cooking anyway, so you may use the utensils." We started immediately. Under close supervision and advice from Kaka who had an efficient system of speed, I managed to teach the cooks about the new style of making sweets. It amazed them that I was not using any milk. But nobody was complaining. We worked straight though the night. I kept them engaged with entertainment, jokes and songs. Ideally, I would have loved to offer them refreshments, but it was a luxury I could not afford.

Early next morning, by the time the store opened, we had the boxes ready and packed. People came in and were pleased to see the packaging. I had added my own twist to the boxes to make them stand out of the ordinary. Things went well. We got more orders for the next few weeks; with the festive time approaching, people wanted to try this new cuisine more and more. After paying Kaka for his resources, I had enough money left over to call it a profitable deal!

A month had passed since my first day, standing outside Kaka's store, offering free modaks to people. We had managed to secure enough orders to keep us busy through the entire festive season. Watching Kaka's success, some other halwais had also asked us to bring the modaks to their stores. With the profit margin we had made on each sale, we now had our own little brand and label in the market. Every evening, the family would get together and make these compact boxes and put a special symbol on top as an elephant carrying a box in his trunk. We picked on the term that the local people had given us. Wherever we went to speak and pitch our modaks, people said that the *MithaiWala* (the sweets man) was here. We thus decided to call ourselves 'MithaiWala'. Our boxes were so designed that you could open them to look like a platter, ready to serve as it is. In this way, when you served the sweets, our name and branding would be visible to anyone eating them!

In the meanwhile, our recycled VR model was up and running for use. People who had travelled through Kailash were taking back sweets to all over the galaxy and our little scan digits on the box made it easy for anyone to view us on the VR portal online and order for more products. The VR allowed them to see the sweets in life-like form, understand its composition and order accordingly. It was not long before our first order was called in from a far-away state in India. As it turns out, people in Maharashtra had been going gaga about the modaks and were eager to place orders. This is where the next challenge of the game began. So far, MithaiWala had been selling things locally. But with distant transportation came a lot of costs and administration issues to ensure that we would deliver only quality product. It was now time to start investing in Research and Development of a packaging and delivery system that would be cost and quality effective. So far, it had been only Chintan, Srijan, Mother Parvati and Uncle Nandi with me, and we had been working hours off the charts to keep the finances rolling. After the last venture, we had taken a lot of time to recover from the financial shock, and thus, with diligent bootstrapping, we were forced to keep our expenses to a bare minimum. I had reduced all my bills to their minimum limit and was spending as thriftily as possible. I sold some of my equipments, including my VR design set-up that had been an expensive splurge from the funding money last time. With some money at hand now, we decided to tie up with 'Globe hopper', the agency run by Narada that he used to transport resources from one end of the universe to another. We built a cheap and efficient system with him to transport bulk orders within limited time to secure the quality of the sweets. We were on the edge of our financial crunch, but the orders were coming up aggressively and we knew that if we played our cards well, we would have money to expand soon. It was time to work on the scale up model now and therefore time to bring more people on-board with the team. After our tie up with 'Globe hopper', on discounted rates, we were managing to get more orders from outside of Kailash and hence, had enough money to keep things rolling for the next six months. I had asked Nandi Uncle to come on-board full time with us to help with the expansion. The next steps would be to take the aggressive move on and capture more clients in the market. With Nandi uncle on board, we could now think about dividing up the team work so we could each work on different verticals.

Things were looking upwards and as more and more brain storming came on, we spent more and more time on building, rejecting and rebuilding ideas of expansion and connecting to more diverse producers to join MithaiWala. It was all a matter of time now.

Moral – With a startup that is finding its foot in the ground, you have to push your limits and try everything that you have reason to believe in. It is in these times when you must not be afraid to take risks, push conventions and prove your worth. What you introduce yourself with is of the most importance and thus, creating a first impression is of top priority. It is important to have your priorities right in terms of attention and investment. But the moment you have found your window and proof of success, it is time to get aggressive while you still have the edge of the first. If that window is missed, you may be overtaken by hawks who copy your model. Ensure that your selling point is unique and relevant for your target audience and once you have figured that out, sky is the limit!

13

Bootstrapping – The nuts and bolts of operations

$\mathcal{I}$ t has been a few months since the operation of our business. I could feel the stress increasing and everything was catching a pace that had us on our edges. My brand of producing and delivering customized and colloquial sweets had been picking up popularity and people from across the galaxies had been actively seeking enquiries, both at the customer, as well as the producers' end. These were good signs, but, as mother Parvati had warned, "These are the best of the times and the worst of the times for you, Ganesha. You have the ability to either put the system into place now, that will set the foundation of an empire of enterprise, or you will cave in under the pressure of the burden that comes with its responsibilities and crash back to the center." I know she did not mean to scare me, but it was important for me to understand the critical position. With the expansion of the operations, I also had to consider the growing desperation for capital. I remember how many decisions had been altered, delayed or compromised with because our priority was to ensure financial security and splurging was neither in my mind nor a luxury that my pocket could afford at that moment. One such decision that had brought the best of our creative genius (as they say, necessity is the mother of all inventions!) was the building up of our brand.

It was around the time when the orders had begun to come in large numbers for different types of sweets and we were in need of a uniform packaging and brand building. "It is not just the packaging, Ganesha; we are beginning to get popular across the planets in the universe. Now is our chance to step up from an anonymous service and build a name that people will remember. Before anyone else gets a chance of taking up this idea and pitch it as a bigger and better form, we have to build ownership to this!" Srijan debated intently with me. I understood his point but wasn't too sure if we could afford that kind of expenditure. However, one idea stuck my head. If we kept it simple and pitched the idea of building collaboration with the producers that we partnered up with, we could reduce packaging cost and co-brand, thus keeping the interest of the producers intact.

When we first began talking to some of the famous sweet makers in our area, they were reluctant in following this system. "Ganesha, my shop is known all over the city and beyond the Kailash for its exquisite sweets. I do not see any sense in losing my own brand value by co-branding with you." I knew this wasn't going to be an easy discussion, but I had come prepared with my arguments. "Mohanji, I know you are popular and have a value that cannot be shadowed by any other brand around you. But you have to understand that there's a specialty that is being portrayed in this product. It is a cuisine that is unique and is being presented in a unique way to people who value it more than the limitations of geography. With this new form of service, you have to allow for a new image to form, otherwise, we will drown into the crowd of being just another name of sweets." I could see that he had stopped to ponder over this argument. I was ready to play my ace now. "You know, these sweets won't last on their own if they have to be transported to a distant land. You know I have the packaging that can sustain the delivery and hold the VR chip that helps with live tracking and information on the product. That is something you will not find anywhere else." I knew I had him.

It didn't take long before we had found a uniform branding mechanism. We called ourselves "The Sweet Post" because we were a delivery that posted the best sweets wherever you wanted. The idea was to be minimalistic and simple. The box would be a simple pink cuboid and on the front side of the box would be the logo of the respective sweet shop. On top would be our branding, along with the chip for people to operate on for further details on the product or other ranges, and for us to enable live tracking and viewing of the delivery from the origin to the end. The boxes ensured optimum temperature and shape for the content inside by fiber lining. After the first few and the most difficult trials of the packaging, it was proved that we would be able to handle the quality we were expecting to deliver with the VR device on.

"Ganesha, the prototype for the front end, even if we keep to our frugal best, will need some hefty investment." Chintan spoke with concern. Now, that was one thing I had learned while going through the biggest financial crunch of my life – efficiency and optimization of everything that is available or even reachable. When we had first begun full scale operation, father had sat me down and evaluated my current status (and I couldn't blame him for being concerned. I had led an enterprise to failure once!) "Ganesha, now that systems are in place more or less, how do you plan to operate with your team without a space to work in?" I had been contemplating about this for a while and making small adjustments within my room and backyard for meetings and storage.

"Father, our home has always been an open space for people across the Universe. All of the nature's biggest plans and strategies have been made right here by you, Brahma and Vishnu. I am sure my humble enterprise will find ample room here to run the basic functionalities. And we will build the next steps as we go along."

He had that pleased smile on his face because I knew he had heard the right words. His fatherly love and advice poured out to me, "You have the wisdom and words to connect and compel anyone, Ganesha, and do not ever forget that as your biggest strength. Use it well." And thus, my office space was formally occupied, with chairs, rugs, mats and stools. It wasn't what you would call a conventional work space, but it was every inch efficient with whatever one needed. My bedroom had become a makeshift office for the team. It was also a makeshift warehouse, a makeshift meeting room and a makeshift bedroom, all depending on the need of the hour. "Besides, it feels like I am working from my own room, I like that comfort!" pointed one of my interns as we sat discussing what we needed to do for the VR modification.

I looked around at this space that had been utilized to the last inch of its limits. "I am sure there's something we can do, we still haven't explored this to its last inch," I said aloud more to myself than to a worried Chintan. It was then that I stumbled upon my old box with the prototype and system of VR of Shrishti, the last enterprise I had tried to run and failed miserably in. "But this is a brilliant idea!" I exclaimed realizing that Chintan had no idea what I had been thinking. All the remains and refuses from Shrishti still had enough potential to be utilized and customized into the necessities for The Sweet Post.

"It may be a lot more work, sure," Chintan responded pondering, "But this will indeed save us a lot more money than I could have imagined. There will, however, be a few expenses at the design end that I may have no control over." I knew there were people who would have to be paid. But I had begun exploring my skills with building trust and compatibility with people in an extraordinary way – one of the perks of failing and learning in business is that when you have seen the worst part, you are willing to do anything to get to the better part! "I will take care of that," I promised Chintan as we planned to retire for the night.

When you are bootstrapping, every little decision comes with a cost that you have to dish out of another share. Where on the one hand, funding is like Kuber's pot of money, you can withdraw as you like from the pot and the pot will always have some spare for later use. Bootstrapping, on the other hand, means spending or rather scratching every penny out of your pocket. Therefore, if new expenses come up, you don't have a budget for them; you negotiate with other expenses, tie your knots even tighter and somehow pull the strings. However, the biggest advantage of bootstrapping is that you run by your rules, you control the course of action, and above all, ownership is yours. The Sweet Post was beginning to build a market base and the most imminent proof of this came in the form of revenue that we had begun to generate within the first month of being officially operational.

The best way to sustain, if you are bootstrapping, is to expand.

It may be scary, but it has to be done, along with diligence and persistence, of course. "Ganesha, we are moving too fast. At this pace, we will not be able to handle the work load, and if something goes wrong, we lose all the hard earned success so far!" Chintan was already getting worked up and when I called for a meeting to look at earth for business development with the intention to start operation outside of Kailash.

"There's the issue of quality control and we do not have enough number of customers to venture into expansion in a distant land."

You cannot let fears determine your route and pace. They should only be seen as signs of information once you choose your path. "There's only one way to find out, Chintan," I spoke reassuringly. "We have to step out of our comfort zone now. The product has been tested, the model is doing well. We would be fools to not act immediately and make the most of pioneering this idea. Otherwise, it won't be long before someone else sweeps in and changes our success into their opportunity." I sounded more confident than I felt, but I was not going to let my team, that now comprised Chintan, Srijan, two interns from the

Management Institute of Milky Way and Nandi Uncle, who was on the advisory team and guided us in business development. His approving nod was encouraging and I explained to the team about my plan of visiting the existing clients and picking on the database provided by existing business partners to begin tapping on newer, wider audience. With this determination, I left for my tour with the agenda of meeting the customers I had been working with for the last few months.

The experience of one on one interaction with the partners was as insightful as it was heart-warming. I gathered information about the challenges they were facing and was able to share the expectations I had with them. "Each box takes about five minutes from beginning to the end," one of the partners told me candidly one evening. "However, when there are bulk orders, the scope of errors increases massively and therefore, more time is needed for correction." We have therefore designed a mechanism that replicates the arrangement of a single order into the number of orders you ask for. The only thing left to do manually then, is to place the items in the box, which takes a lot less time when the arrangement has been determined in advance. I was struck by the sheer simplicity and brilliance of the idea. The logic behind had been simple and effective and yet, it could help save hours on bulk orders. With a detailed conversation, I found out that the problem that he was facing, and by the looks of it, other partners would be facing too was not knowing in advance how much order was expected, and thus not being able to calculate their preparation. "It is ironical because our over-all demand and supply algorithm roughly remains the same each month," I mentioned recalling the data of the last quarter. "Perhaps, if I work out a plan to show how much each of the partners are producing and delivering, the algorithm can also reveal the remaining share of the month's quota, thus giving you a fair warning about expectancy. What do you think?"

By his expressions, I could tell that he was dazed. "Well, as long as you can figure out the math of it, I will be happy to know."

Many such revelations came to light and many connections were formed and reformed through these personal visits. With every hand shake and every response, I was taken back to the memory of childhood, watching father Shiva leaving with his heard of aghoris to travel around for months altogether. I remember father leaving for *rath yatra* with his *'gadh'* of followers in the auspicious month of Sawan when he would travel all around the universe. "Why does he leave, Ma?" Kartikey and I would ask. "Does he not like it here in Kailash, with us?" Mother would smile with us lovingly and answer, "He loves you and Kailash a lot, Ganesha. That is why he wants to make sure that nothing goes wrong anywhere and so he can make everything better for you and for all his people."

All that made sense now. You take care of your environment and the environment takes care of you in return. Through several promotional meetings and personal engagements with my partners, I had managed to set up a bond of faith and understanding. Wherever I went, I carried a mixed bag of 'The Sweet Post'. Wherever it was possible, I engaged in activities that promoted local or homemade cuisines and especially sweets in solidarity with colloquial producers. It was with these personal interactions, feedback and follow up with all my customers that 'The Sweet Post' started building a reputation of being the people's brand. A lot of time was spent in establishing the feedback mechanism and setting up a system that enabled us to be accessible and available. Unlike the whole 'wish center' rage that was storming the universe, with its call center version especially popular in India, we decided that a dedicated team would handle front end communication for B2B and B2C in house. "Not only does this save us money, but also ensures that quality of communication is within monitoring reach," Nandi Uncle had pointed out when he made the suggestion for the first time. It was another insightful lesson learned; it is easy to outsource, always. But you have to decide whether you want easy or good! With the increasing work load, the team size also considerably expanded and from four, we soon turned to a crew of twelve.

Deep in my thought one day, I found myself looking for ways to advertise, however, the cost of mass communication is no enigma. We desperately needed to popularize, but the burns from the last trial had told us better than going all in for marketing and advertising. "Back in my days, the only advertising was a good quality and a good mouth," Narada spoke one day as father Shiva, mother Parvati and I sat with him during one of his visits to Kailash. "Look at me. I travel across galaxies, choose my audience and speak to them in a language they will understand. My communication enterprise has never had to waste money in publicity because we are our own adverts." His words made perfect sense. There were so many people I knew and so many people who mother and father worked with across the geography. All I had to do was start reaching out to them with my product and convince them to become the brand ambassadors. I reached out to Goddess Saraswati to use 'The Sweet Post' in her innovation classes as reward goodies I also managed to connect with Lakshmi and convince her into offering 'The Sweet Post' snacks in her VC meetings! Right there, with hard work and close to negligible cost was our own little advertisement happening by the most influential creatures of the universe.

It was also around this time that I was asked by Goddess Lakshmi to accompany her to the Universal Entrepreneurial Conference and I did meet some venture capitalists there who took interest in round B funding. Fortunately for us, we do not need capital desperately anymore and so, with deliberation along with my team, I managed to decline the offers and continued bootstrapping. Chintan, however, held very different opinions. He insisted that they take up the funding since it will help to ease the load.

"The crisis that the team has been through in the past is not hidden from you, Ganesha," he said. "We have held back from several entrepreneurial luxuries that we would be able to afford if the funding sails through." I understood his exhaustion. Chintan had after all helped to manage all the finances and crunched numbers day in and day out to make sure that we stayed afloat.

"I know that the possibilities seem tempting. We have been working on the edge for a while now and it only feels well deserved that we allow ourselves the liberty of spending in a way that we deserve. However, it is with a lot of hard work that we have been able to achieve this strength and independence and it will be such a loss to allow ourselves to be swayed by glamour at the brink of our success." The road ahead would be uphill. With ambitions rising, pressure building and goals expanding, I will have many stars to plead to, many constellations to consider before my dreams of standing as a successful and independent entrepreneur, away from the shadows of being a failure or a dream come true.

Moral – Bootstrapping is a challenge that, if embarked, will show you a million shades of an enterprise. It requires meticulous observation of the most minute details and extra efforts into ensuring that the front and back end connections are strong. What cannot be compensated by money is built by efforts, especially with personal communication and creating an understanding of the perspective of the other end of the business. Maintaining a quality that becomes its own brand is what sets you apart in this world of hoarding ideas. Innovation is what sets you apart from the hoard of people before and after you, and it is this innovation that should keep you on your edge, with constant effort to contextualize and customize developments, depending on what the trends are. Unfortunately, (or fortunately) there are no footsteps to follow when you run a startup; you can follow your own rules since each startup has its own conventions, experiments and priorities. Remember that risks are important, but you should bring yourself to a position first where you can take risks and then dive in. Once that confidence has been achieved, success will follow suit. Be creative, push yourself without compromise and never, ever, settle into your comfort zone.

14

To Hire is Human: Human Resources in bootstrapping

There are many stories that float around in the Dev Lok that I used to wonder upon their mysteries. For instance, there were times when the gods and goddesses would come together for events. However, there would always be some who could not be teamed up with others. "Why are they so incompatible with each other, Father?" I would ask. "This is not incompatibility, son. This is what keeps the world in a balance. When one element gets on the side of excess, the other sides have to even out somehow. This is the rule of the cosmos. The gods, that represent all elements of life, also need to equalize with their presence or absence.

Did you know that Lakshmi and Saraswati share the same equation? Wherever Saraswati, the power of knowledge goes, Lakshmi, wealth follows inadvertently. However, whenever Lakshmi tries to get very close, Saraswati escapes! This is how the system works. Be mindful of the money you earn, Ganesha.

If it is wealth alone that you are after, then that is easy to find. But if you seek prosperity, remember to use your intellect more than your pocket." This could not be any truer and relevant given my circumstances. 'The Sweet Post' had begun making a decent amount of revenue and the model had been established as viable. Thus, the second round of expansion had to be initiated first of all into geographical diversion and eventually into product range. I had gone to Saraswati at this time to get some insight at her startup incubation center on the advice of Mother Parvati. "That is where all the ideas begin, nothing sprouts without her presence," mother had said nudging. This is one thing that no degree or classrooms will teach you, the tales of experience. Whenever possible, meet more people, learn from them and look for insights between the lines.

"When you cannot afford luxurious associations, time and sincerity are your best investments," Saraswati had told me in answer to the question about financial management. "There will be several options of good quality services available if you want to pay a price. But if you want the best quality, no money can buy it. There are means to work around expenses through intellect."

There is a straight equation between quality and people. Which is why, the best organizations have the best people working for them. When I say best, I mean most relevant. There are incredible people stuck in wrong jobs and are not able to realize their correct potential. It is that is why imperative to assess the right needs of human resources in your organization and only hire people most suitable for most specific jobs. During one of my conversations with Lord Krishna, who is known as a people's person, I found out some insight about the best strategies of working with people. "I have to deal with innumerable people on a daily basis, with a diverse range of potentials and skills," he told me at one of the Pilgrimage Conventions in Kailash. Many gods and goddesses come together to watch the pilgrimage exhibitions in the mountain where thousands of humans visit every year. It is here that stalls are set up for recruitment, skill development and outsourcing of assignments are done because the best mix of people comes together. "Before you hire anyone, Ganesha, you have to know exactly what you want them to do. Every single resource in your startup is an expense first and an asset second. It is therefore imperative to have clearly defined roles, scopes, deliverables and compensations for each individual. Needless to say, to have HR management is a herculean responsibility to ensure that not only do you have the right people, but so that you are the right organization for them and that their purpose is served in the intended way!" Krishna's words made perfect sense. I had been looking for people in terms of manpower, but I had to focus more on forming strategic alliance with each and every person that came onboard. It is like building a machine with individual levers, nuts, wheels and circuits, etc. The machine may look like one giant unit, but it has to be made of perfectly fitting pieces that work with one another and are in principle, aligned with the bigger mechanism of the machine. This is exactly what human resource management is about.

But how do we get this strategy working for human resources when we are bootstrapped and working on the edge of our expenses? Simple – by incorporating low cost resources into a high performing system. First and foremost, the focus should be on right recruitment. Instead of hiring high end professionals for full time jobs, we decided to turn to freelance contract talents. Instead of looking for conventionally well-established professionals, we went for new and innovative minds fresh out of college or those still pursuing their out of the box dreams.

"The best thing to look in people is what they want to bring to the table, not what they are expected to follow," Nandi Uncle told me before our first round of interviews. "There will always be people who join an organization for money. But they are not the best choice for you, especially as a bootstrapping startup. What you need is people with a vision and passion and people who are not shy of taking risks, just like you!" This made a lot of sense and inspired me to look for youngsters across universities, for portfolios online with out of the box ideas and for freelance consultants who had worked with people I know. This served many purposes. First of all, I knew they were already in the making and therefore, not completely molded into conventional thought processes. This would enable them to think out of the box and work with their own discretion instead of following the curve that long professional years teach you. Second of all, these would be people whose work is available for observation and assessment, thus I am completely aware of their capability, not just in verbal claims, but actual, physical or at least virtual display. Third, working with people who come from known contacts and recommendations always adds an advantage of credibility and accountability. This means a lot in the world where inexperience and deceit causes more financial damage than anything else. Reliability comes with its perks that take you a long way, especially in a bootstrapped startup where the stakes are already very high. Thus, with these points in mind, I began with my search for people, young and old, qualified or passionate, to come on board with The Sweet Post. I especially sought young men and women who had exhibited examples of leadership and initiatives.

As a result of my diligent search, through every contact, every recommendation, every connection and every institution, we found out a batch of young interns, trainees and some freelance workers who could work with us remotely and join us through VR once a day for in-person discussions. Most of these trainees, although lacking in experience, had great intuition and were very willing to learn. One may have heard many times that baby-sitting is a strict no-no in a space with money and time crunch. However, I felt that this was a great opportunity to start with fresh minds and to give them responsibilities with the team so that they get ample exposure to learn and yet, sufficient space to experiment and show initiative. Did I mention the best part? Such talent is generally available at a lower cost, and though you spend time with them a lot more than a well-played professional, you reap financial as well as operational benefits two-fold! One thing I have learnt over time, with both my success as well as my rebirth into entrepreneurship, is that you have to identify your strength and make the best use of it. If you do not do that, you simply waste the reason you exist in the first place. "You are great with people, never let that skill go wasted," Mother Parvati had reminded me repeatedly. And that lesson, I carried with me every single day, with people, irrespective of their position or relation with me. I began spending more and more time with the trainees and interns. It is amazing to see the kind of ideas and perspectives they can bring to light as opposed to your own.

With regular and rigorous brainstorming, you can streamline the goals and expectations, define self-proclaimed targets and ensure that there is a continuous learning curve with each and every person, irrespective of their roles in the organization. Once I knew that my team was built around the skeleton of a strong system, I could begin focusing on individual departments of finance, innovation, operation, customer service, quality control and HR management. Srijan, Chintan, Nandi Uncle and I personally overlooked these departments and held daily interaction sessions to make sure that everyone was in sync, both in planning and in actions.

However, with innovative minds came creative clashes and challenges too. There are different ideas that often bring out operational challenges. However, with brainstorming and strategic organization, a cordial system can be set up to deal with this. "Why don't you split targets with teams? Creating an internal competitive and incentivized environment helps to channel creativity and subjectivity into a productive and ever growing format," Nandi Uncle had been working with people across the universe with father Shiva and had his own share of learning that helped with deal with people of all kinds, all skill sets and all methodology of work. This worked like magic.

We split teams and gave them different groups of clients and regions. There were live markers set up to track progress in each of the regions that helped us watch over their developments and experiments. "This is fantastic. I have the teams on hot line and I get notifications if there is any activity beyond or below the regular band width. It is great to allow them the space for competitive aggression for achievements and yet, if things get risky or potentially downhill, I get notifications well in advance to rectify the orders before it is too late," Chintan was telling me in one of our monthly review discussions.

The teams nodded with sincere agreement. "I like that you give us the space to keep trying our skills and that means a lot to our confidence," said one of the trainees during the same meeting. These were good signs. With time, the error alerts reduced more and more while regional success rates grew many folds.

There is a certain edge you hold as a startup if you are an innovator in a field that does not have many competitors. Not only do you have a head start, but you have tried and tested several aspects of it and therefore, you know which tracks lead to the wrong milestones and which ones are the best routes to take against upcoming challenges. With the confidence and stability we had managed to achieve with our team, we decided to take innovative competitiveness to the next level.

"We introduce quarterly experiment challenge. You come up with a working and proven model of innovation with universal application value and if you win, not only does your experiment get adopted all through The Sweet Post. But you also win collective bonus for the quarter for your team!" Srijan announced at the new quarter's beginning. I could see some apprehensions, as are always there when something new is introduced into an existing system. But I thought to give it half a year's time before making a decision. That is another take away from having worked with a bunch of new ideas and risks in your pocket. You have to give things time and patience. You set yourself a capped timeline to try the concept, but within that time frame, you do not doubt the actions, you do not cross your determination and above all, you keep your eyes and ears open with observation. This is exactly what we did for half a year and six months down the line, we were three models richer and six team bonds healthier than before this experiment!

Several challenges will pop us despite the most stringent cautions and most liberal cultures maintained in your enterprise. The biggest one you encounter around working with freelancers, interns or trainees is that they will leave, inadvertently, no matter how hard you try. There is nothing to be disappointed about in this or even shocked. When it comes to machines, models or money, the unit is predictable, stable and sustainable. "But no human being is a hundred percent consistent and static, that is what makes them human," Saraswati had spoken to me in one of our evening walks at her incubation center. "That is why, you can never be fool proofed of human resource faults." But what can be done for minimum damage and most efficient recovery when such faults occur? I had to dig deep to understand human resource management. "Do what you do best, set up systems. People may change, but systems will remain like a constant guideline to help you recover from the change." That made sense. We had to get our modules, policies and most importantly, our incubation and orientation platforms into an effective and efficient format. With attrition rates hitting us mildly, although at least not devastatingly, as compared to other organizations, we needed a swift program to bring in replacements and to orient them into fully functional status in the least amount of time. It was thus decided to use our VR system to set up an archive of activities, challenges, accomplishments and decisions made in each process and the same was used for orientation with the help of an 'anchor' who was responsible for mentoring any new appointee. The best way of making sure that this system works efficiently is by monitoring the progress at month end and incentivizing the mentor as well as the trainee for optimum performance. "It always helps to set high standards. Exhibit excellence to expect excellence," was the motto I took away from Brahma's creative genius. He has never settled for anything less than the best in each of his tech-designs. And by doing so, he has set such a benchmark that anyone who associated himself with Brahma automatically knows what level of supremacy is expected out of their performance. In short, compromise for nothing less than excellence, in the most basic culture of your organization. After this standard has been set, you, your team and the associated partners will all be aware of the expectations and strive accordingly. As Brahma said himself, "It is not just about the product you make, but the environment you set up that makes you a brand of excellence!"

There are times when you rely on your team more than your friends or sometimes, even your family. This reliance goes a long way with financial, social and even emotional stability that you may provide and seek in the ecology of entrepreneurship. "Not everything comes with a price, Ganesha," Sarawasti had told me one day when I asked her about her cordial relation with Lakshmi, "You need money for business, but you need wisdom and relations for success." The kind of culture and principles you set with your team decides how they treat you and pledge their loyalty. You can either be a white collared team with desks and lunch boxes or a family that dines together and stands for each other, no matter what. Human resource has a big element of 'human' in it and it is entirely up to you how you determine which human qualities you prioritize.

There were times in the past where I had looked for degrees and status to decide what people stand for. This was a time when I was myself looking for glamorous labels to associate myself with. However, I now know that passion stands above everything else. If you find someone who really needs an opportunity, hire them. I am not talking about quaint collection of good 'karma' or doing looking after the larger good. But if a person in need comes on board with your principle, not only have you brought employment, but you have found someone whose loyalties and commitment will hardly ever need any questioning or evaluation. Lessons can be learnt, labels can be printed and erased with time. However, passion, need and dedication only come to those who are hungry enough for it. A big part of human resource management was my share of lessons learnt with people who made up with dedication and sincerity what they lacked in qualifications. Till date, I have never had a chance to review my decision of hiring them, let alone feeling a hint of regret! With the most human element of human resources on your side, the sky is your limit, and the stars beyond, your guiding light.

Moral – Human resources are the trigger point that can make or break your enterprise. Not only is this element the most cost consuming aspect that comes as a price of expansion, but also responsible for implementation of your dreams. Diligent and wise assessment of the right people for the right job can be a game changer. However, instead of looking for the 'right' people in the shelves of brands, look for passion, proven talent (if not experience) and alignment with your philosophy; only that is the perfect recipe of a star employee. Encouraging healthy competition and team work helps to smooth operations and prevent clashes of interest. It is always wise to delegate responsibilities and inculcate spirit of leadership and initiatives. While management is advised, it is in the best interest for a sustainable development in the organization to allow space for experiments, ingenuities and decision making amidst employees. Allowing team members to associate with each other and to work on collective incentivizing not only works as a motivation factor, but also ensures cooperative ambience instead of individualistic interests. Choose wisely, stay connected, incentivize and encourage accomplishments. Remember, business is as much made of people as it is made of money.

15

When Victory Brings Rewards:
Super entrepreneur was born

*F*orever in the revolution of the universe, galaxies converge and divide. Forever, stars die as black holes or are born as shining twinkles. The entire creation is far too big to be bothered by an individual's failure or success and yet, we strive towards that which we claim to be our success, dodging all challenges and battling all struggles that the universe throws in our paths. Some of these successes go down in history as exemplary achievements, for others to learn and follow. And today is one such day when I am about to become a small part of the big history of success for those who have come before me have taught me to work hard and fight without giving up.

After having struggled through a boulevard of challenges and failures, I had finally found myself walking on the right track. Do not get me wrong, it was neither a hidden path in the forest that I just happened to discover, nor a stream I stumbled upon while turning a corner. It was a diligent, calculated and determined execution of learnings, strategies and definitely mistakes that taught me to do the right thing. It has been essential to keep all the nuts and bolts of entrepreneurship close by because, and I know this from experience, that you will need them at some point in your journey. The last couple of years have been like sailing through high and low tides. The very first struggle was about dealing with failure and watching my confidence and hard work crash with the failure. From there on, finding the right product in the right market also posed as a challenge. Onward in the journey, dealing with people, analyzing strategic moves, working on finances also came as valuable lessons. However, as the outward journey progressed with new learnings, new skills and strengths, an inward journey also came through with more knowledge about my own capabilities, my strengths and weaknesses. This helped me in stretching my boundaries and molding my own actions and words in a form that was most appropriate for my environment. The world of enterprise has its financial and glamorous rewards, but above all, it brings you the jewels of patience, humility and acceptance and these take you forward in the long run, both professionally as well as personally. With all these experiences, I stand on this podium desk, delivering my address of gratitude where I have tried to share with you as openly and honestly my story of both failure and success, naivety and nobility, challenges and choices, not just as a means to redeem my pride, but because this is all I have to offer to everyone, so they may take their own picks from my learnings and make use of my mistakes in their own route to the world of entrepreneurship.

Many of you must have understood my agony when it came to setting a stable and sustainable system into my startup so that we can get over the daily nuances of operations and focus our energy on bigger and better things. If we unthread the beads backwards, this stage of success reverts to establishing a humble yet effective team as a family, preceded by the financial backbone and its management for a bootstrapped enterprise. Even before we started playing with big money, all our attention was focused on building the right business with the right people and that required an immense amount of one on one interactions with both our partners as well as the consumer end to understand and evaluate each stage of the process flow, to identify the loop holes and bottle necks, to highlight the strengths and to have a strong control over the entire machinery of The Sweet Post. The gods from across the universe are famous or rather infamous for travelling more often than not! It happens so often that you try to book an appointment with them or seek some advice through hotlines and their network is unavailable. Isn't that true? But it is not that they are unavailable, wandering around aimlessly or for leisure. They travel with specific agenda, for evaluation of their respective progress, for challenges in their departments and for the purpose of eliminating any confusion that may have arisen due to communication gaps. So every time you think that the gods of water, or clouds or food or prosperity are unavailable, you are most likely not looking in the right place for them. Follow their examples, pursue evaluations in your own route and you will, sooner or later, meet them again!

In my own journey of evaluation, I have found the significance of prioritizing my goals, especially when they are related to financial decisions. There will be some short-term targets and some long term goals that need categorical differentiation and you need to either choose or place them in chronology of execution. I can tell you this as a bootstrapping startup because we have often been short on cash and one thing I learned was that you do not necessarily have to build new roads for every single operational development. Remember that there's always a tunnel waiting to be dug inside a hill that can connect different roads together. More often than not, entrepreneurial success will demand innovation, risks and bending the conventions, and although it may seem dicey, you will have to take the plunge if you want to see the light at the end of the tunnel.

I took my plunge sometime back when the business of The Sweet Post had kicked off considerably and we had become profitable at an appreciable scale. It was here that we were looking to diversify and set up office spaces in five different galaxies and needed to take out a huge chunk of our profit for circulation. It was around then that I was approached by a leading business magazine to give an interview for their startup special edition. I had been voted amongst the top ten rising entrepreneurs of the Galaxy, but I was nervous about this public appearance. "There is nothing that a modak cannot charm," my father, Shiva had joked the evening before the interview. "As long as you speak with honesty and passion, people will love your words... of course, the plate of modak does the rest!" he joked. Father would often joke with me and tell me about all the silly things he used to do when he was setting up his empire in Kailash. I think this was his way to calm down my nerves and assure me that despite the mistakes, you can allow yourself the liberty to celebrations of all the hard work you have done. "Make sure you celebrate and thank all the people who have helped you get where you are." I smiled humbly, well aware of the role that my team has played in not only the work they do, but the support they have become in this journey.

There were many milestones that followed that interview. Being featured amongst the top ten rising entrepreneurs, getting published in social media and online magazines that have a wider audience, being invited for my very own virtual reality feature in the universal studio… these were some of the achievements that had many doors opening for us. "I can finally breathe freely, Ma," I had expressed my heart's relief to mother Parvati one day. I can see that we are on the right track now." But there were still choices that made me sleepless at nights. Should I accept Venture Capital offers and allow my team some breathing space that I know they deserve? Should I work on rebranding now that we have achieved a whole new scale of consequence? Which products should I continue with, which should I eliminate? These were questions that are never answered in a book. There is not one expert in the universe who will come and make these decisions for you. It happens so often that we close our eyes and ask the powers above us to do certain things for us, but if you look deeper and closer, you are the one who has to actually lift your head, open your eyes and work towards your wish, the powers then work as the headlights in front of your engine, showing you the path as you go! Instead of looking for rule books or ideas for inspiration, you should work thoroughly on your knowledge so that you have the confidence about the nuts and bolts of your product. When you have that, you will be able to take the risk of experimentation and that leads to the discovery of the best product permutation with trial and error. Without mistakes, there will be no learnings and without those, you will not know what works and what does not. However, it is equally important to realize and accept when you are going wrong and to stop with minimum damage without hesitation.

Today, I stand before you all with fifteen branches and 50 sub-centres of The Sweet Post all over the universe. There are sponsors pursuing us to find co-branding on our boxes. Delivery portals want to collaborate with us because we make up a massive share in the business. The biggest names you may have heard are our brand ambassadors or endorsers. Our share value is under top fifty and it has been only a couple of years since we rolled into operation! Do not get me wrong though. Everything I just told you is not a back patting from the mouth of an arrogant new blood who has come to throne suddenly and does not know how to handle his attitude. The only reason why I narrate this 'success story' is because I want you to know the naked truth about enterprises. I want you to understand the nuances of every step all the way from the bottom to the top. I want you to identify the challenge it takes to rise from a makeshift, work from home office into a multi-location organization. I want you to know the relief of having to stand outside a shop to hand out free samples to reaching a point where people set appointments with you with the hope that you will agree to associate with them. I would implore you to see how the journey works from no one knowing you to you becoming the brand that even the most famous find involvement with. I want you to see what it takes in the struggle of everyday budget cuts to reaching a turnover that is sufficient to feed more than eight hundred mouths and still continue to grow business every year. Most importantly, I want you to understand that after a plethora of challenges, comes a time when you find stability; it is just a matter of holding on till the tide calms down. With all of this, I want you to believe in the common man's dream. I had what most of you would have or can manage to build with due diligence. No capital to speak for, no experience in conventional definitions. Neither did I have an ancestral luxury to carry forward, nor an environment that promoted the kind of risks that I had taken at my stage. I was just as filled with fears and anxiety as the next door neighbour. Most important of all, I made mistakes and plenty of them too. I spent money in the wrong place, failed miserably in my first attempt, continued to make mistakes even later, until I did not make them anymore. I can only boast of average intelligence, I have not had premium education and neither have I been brought up around incubating business minded stalwarts who could teach me the trade. In fact, I did not even know I wanted to be an entrepreneur until one day it struck me that I did! The only thing that I did know was that once I had begun, I was not going to turn back and that every step of the way, I would seek everything I could find, to the last bits of my capacity. I befriended when I had to and chose alienation when that was required of me. I cried for help and I put a strong foot down when the situation demanded. I scratched every surface, dug up every contact, exploited every window of an opportunity and left nothing untouched. Above all, I took baby steps and let the humble light of faith glow in my heart. There were times when I thought I wouldn't make it, sure. But these were the times I pushed the hardest and paid the most attention to make sure that I did not let this feeling win.

What is the difference between a regular man with a job and me, you ask? When you work for entrepreneurial development, you stop thinking about yourself and your horizon widens magnanimously. Every decision you make affects not just one person but thousands of families. And that is why, you learn to work with the families. When you have crossed the stage of 'my idea, my model, my system', you become a whole universe, one with the people who work with you (and not for you). That is the one takeaway for me in this journey. I have found a lot more than I have given. In each and every member, in their own struggles and insights, in people who left and those who did not leave, I found lessons worth learning and bonds worth sharing. Once you have the support and confidence of the people you work with, there is a sense of relief, an invisible cushion that tells you that someone always has your back! I turn around and look into the crowd and I see people with smiles on their face, tears in their eyes and I know they know… the people I speak about hear me loud and clear. That is the kind of bond you earn, and that is what sets you apart.

For those of you who have been following my story closely, you will know that after my first few lessons of failure, I had learned that it is alright to make mistakes, as long as you are keeping your eyes open and willing to identify your mistakes and learn from them. Most of us keep our egos as high as lofty Kailash. But I advise you to keep your ears as large and your nose as flexible as the mighty elephant. Do not be shy of testing every idea that you envisage to develop. Do not hesitate in experimenting with a small pilot if you think something has a potential of expansion. It may seem troublesome, but there is a reason why there are trial rooms in large showrooms. Never dive nose deep into the open sea without first searching for rocks! Once you have assessed the viability of your product or service, not only will it give you the confidence to start with aggressive expansion, but also ensure your knowledge about the hurdles you may face, the reactions you can expect and the choices you can employ in best and worst case scenarios. Keep your steps simple, with your foothold strong on the ground, and your vision focused on your larger goals. It is easy to get distracted, believe me when I say that, because there will be several ideas that pop up once you open the Pandora's Box of the brain's creativity. But you have to use your discretion, keep a close check on what is necessary and what is a diversion away from the alignment of your specific goals. When you follow these simple and basic fundamentals, there is nothing that will stop you from finding your route to success. The rest is intuition, conviction and dedication.

There was a time where I had to struggle desperately to find an audience amidst those who have achieved a lot and are known for their wealth and wisdom. Yet, today, you place me as their equal, with the same respect. I am seated here, honored with Lakshmi and Saraswati, who embody wealth and knowledge. I have come to realize that my position of prosperity and wisdom would not be either possible or even relevant without the presence of these two embodiments. Today, with this award of the title of prosperity, you have not only given me a state of memorable success, but also given every person an idol to look upon when they seek to begin something new and challenging, for I hope I stand as a reminder for you all to continue on your journey with wisdom and perseverance, to have all your hurdles removed with ease and to always find the blessings of knowledge and wealth by your side.

Ganesha was henceforth awarded a position with Lakshmi and Sarawasti as a universal example of the perfect combination for success. It was declared and widely accepted that the worship of any one of the three idols would be incomplete without the other, and above all, for his exemplary display of wisdom, for his spirit of overcoming challenges and for his undying spirit of generosity, Ganesha would be the first one to be remembered in the world of enterprises. Even today, his story is the first that comes to mind, that is first narrated and first announced when people begin with a new venture, as his wisdom is the spirit that clears the path off any challenges, making way for success. Till date, Lakshmi, Ganesha and Saraswati run a successful partnership in many joint ventures. They run their own individual companies and have helped out many budding enterprises, young or old, in finding their own paths to success. Ganesha's name is often advertised across the universe as a reminder for things that can be achieved, if the right trail is chosen.

Moral – You have to cross several stages of doubts, fears, decisions, persuasions, acceptance and elevation in the journey of building a successful enterprise. You will have to let go of apprehensions and come out of your comfort zone to find out what you are good at and what you can make the best of. In the entrepreneurial journey, you should be prepared to scratch every resource available and knock on every contact without being shy of the consequences. Once you know you are on the right track, do not hesitate from being vocal and aggressive with the growth and possession in the market. There is a critical moment of pushing your business when it has proven its quality to you and it is then that you must go all in, operationally and financially, to play the winning strike. Remember, success is not a pedestal reached with magical swish of the wand. It is a step by step process that is achieved with diligence and determination.